CHANCE

Encounters

J. STERLING

<u>DEDICATION</u>

This book is dedicated to anyone who has been lucky enough to find their soulmate in this world... and everyone who has been blessed enough to recognize them.

J. STERLING

♡ CONTENTS

J. STERLING

♡ One

The musical ringtone blared, echoing off the cathedral ceiling and hardwood floor of the apartment Caroline shared with her boyfriend. Tracey's gorgeous smile shone brightly on her cell phone screen.

"He's dead, Caroline. Oh God, Johnny's dead!" Tracey sobbed.

Caroline dropped the phone; her heart pounding as her body began to tremble. She quickly reached down to pick it back up and stammered, "What happened? How?"

"He was off-roading that stupid dirt bike and he lost control or something. I don't know the whole story yet. The funeral's on Thursday, Caroline...you'll come, right?"

"Of course I'll come." Caroline thought back to their freshman year in college when Johnny lived across from them in the co-ed dorms.

Tracey continued to cry and Caroline held it together the best she could.

When they hung up, Caroline grabbed her laptop and dropped onto the couch, wishing she could disappear completely into it. She attempted to search for flights online but was unable to stop her gaze from drifting to photos from college scattered around her apartment. Tears fell a little harder when she realized there would never be any new pictures of Johnny.

She heard the apartment door swing open and her boyfriend, Clay Matthews walked in. Caroline looked up briefly and observed his loosened tie and disheveled dark, wavy hair.

It looks rugged. And hot. Leave it be, she would tell him with a smile whenever he started to fuss the messy strands back into their proper place.

She watched Clay's gorgeous full smile quickly fade and the indents on his cheeks where dimples were supposed to live, but didn't, disappear as his eyes met hers. He dropped his briefcase and car keys onto the wooden floor and rushed over to her, his face drawn with worry.

"Baby, what's wrong? What happened?"

"It's Johnny. He's dead." Her face reddened.

"What? How? What happened?" Clay pulled her into his arms and kissed her damp face.

"I don't know. There was an accident with his dirt bike. That's all Tray told me."

"Shit. When's the funeral?"

"Thursday." She glanced up at him. "That is, if I can find a freaking flight."

"Scoot over. Let me do that for you." Clay gently removed the computer from Caroline's lap.

"Thanks."

"Do you need me to check if I can take time off?" Clay asked suddenly. "I should probably go too."

"No, no. It's okay. You have work and it will be good for me to spend some time alone with Tray."

"Thanks, baby." He placed a kiss on her cheek. "So, when do you want to come back?"

"I was thinking that I'd rather leave Monday morning instead of Sunday night. Do you mind?"

"Not at all. You should definitely stay until Monday. This sucks. He was a really good guy. His poor mom." He hugged her tightly before he tipped her face up to his and kissed her salty lips.

Caroline's thoughts drifted back to when she first met Clay at a social gathering for incoming freshmen. While Caroline introduced herself to every new person she could find, Clay stood alone and simply watched the interactions. When Caroline reached Clay, she remembered thinking how he wasn't cute like the other boys, but handsome.

The memory faded as her cell phone rang once again. "Hey, Tray. I'm looking at a flight that gets in at five. And I'd stay until Monday morning. That's okay, right? Okay. See you in a couple days. I love you, too."

"How's she doing?" Clay asked.

"She's...Tracey, you know? Can't. Stop. Crying," Caroline said as she attempted a smile, but her mouth wouldn't cooperate.

"I can only imagine."

Caroline walked to the hall closet and returned with an armful of photo boxes. She immediately scattered pictures on the floor around her.

Clay watched her organize the photos into piles. "Babe, I'm going to jump in the shower, okay?"

She barely moved or acknowledged his question. "Okay," she muttered.

Caroline allowed herself to get lost in thought once again. She smiled at how lucky she was to have a wonderful boyfriend whom she admired and an internship at a well-respected marketing firm. Her life seemed perfect. Although losing one of her closest friends was the furthest thing from perfect.

She imagined her eventual wedding to Clay and mourned when she realized Johnny wouldn't be there. He would never be a part of any upcoming events or activities. She could barely wrap her mind around that reality. How could she think of a future that didn't include Johnny when he was a part of every future plan she made?

With her heart hurting, she curled into a ball on the floor, surrounded by memories of the not-so-distant past that suddenly seemed like lifetimes ago. She tucked her arms up under her head and sobbed herself to sleep.

****

When Clay stepped out of the shower and into the chilly hallway, he noticed his heartbroken girlfriend asleep on the floor. She had been so beautiful earlier when she was crying, her green eyes glowing like emeralds, and Clay had wanted to tell her then how beautiful she looked, but knew it wasn't the right time.

Clay sighed, guilt consuming him at how relieved he was that Caroline didn't ask him to go to the funeral with her. He was in the middle of helping out with his firm's biggest criminal case to date and there was no way he could leave. He knew he'd never get hired on at the firm if he took time off when it wasn't a matter of life or death. Immediate family's life or death, anyway.

He walked over to where she lay curled on the floor, and crouched down to watch her sleep. He reached out to stroke her hair and thought back to the day they had met. Clay had been drawn to Caroline immediately. Her Southern California beach girl look—with her long, sun-streaked blonde hair, green eyes, and sun-kissed face—reminded him of home.

They'd become so close since then, especially since moving in together after college. Aside from work, this girl was his life.

He gently scooped her up in his arms and settled her on top of their bed. He placed a blanket over her and kissed the top of her head before he closed the bedroom door behind him.

T w o

Caroline's flight landed right on time. Tracey waited for her outside of the baggage claim area in her car. Caroline ran toward the dark blue Jeep Grand Cherokee. The trunk popped open and she tossed her luggage in before running around to the front. Tracey was in the driver's seat, her short blonde hair in perfect order and her blue eyes glowing. The girls hugged and their joy at seeing each other again quickly dissolved into tears over the loss of one of their best friends.

"You look amazing." Caroline's voice hitched as she settled back in her seat after hugging Tracey over the console.

"So do you."

"I can't believe I'm back here for this. I never imagined…" Caroline's voice trailed off. She loved going to school in New York. The city was so alive, vibrant, and full of so many types of people. Living there for five years had given her a perspective she was certain she couldn't have gained anywhere else. She liked what living in New York had done for her soul. She loved being back, just not under these circumstances.

"At least you get to leave," Tray mumbled under her breath, as she glanced over her shoulder before pulling out into traffic.

"What do you mean?" Caroline's face crinkled in confusion.

"Well, you get to leave after it's all over. I have to stay here and run into our old friends, or Johnny's mom. I hate you."

"You could always come back with me, you know?" Caroline's face lit up. "Oh dear God, Tray, please. Please come back with me!" she begged.

"Whatever. You have Clay. You don't need me hanging around all third wheel-esque."

"Clay's never home. He probably wouldn't even notice that you moved in for weeks," Caroline teased.

"You don't mind though, right?" Tracey looked serious. "That he's always gone?"

Caroline smiled. "Are you kidding? I love being home alone."

"Watching reality TV without the sarcastic injections?"

"Among other things...but YES!" The girls giggled. "And I have Bailey, so that's a plus."

"I always forget that Bailey's there," Tracey remembered.

"She said to tell you hi by the way," Caroline smiled.

"Ooh, tell her I said hi back! I'm so happy you have her there."

Caroline laughed. "You're so weird."

"What? Why am I weird? You're the weird one." Tracey glanced quickly to her right and then back to the road. "I still don't know how you can just move from city to city without freaking out. You didn't know anyone when you moved to New York and you didn't even care. Just thinking about that makes me start sweating!"

"See? You're the weird one." Caroline swatted at Tracey's arm.

"Stop. You're going to make me crash!" Tracey's lips curled into a snarl.

Crash.

Memories of Johnny instantly consumed Caroline's every thought. "Tray," Caroline took a long breath. "I am so not looking forward to this."

Tracey looked at her and then quickly looked away. "Tell me about it." She wiped at her face with the back of her free hand. "Are you going to speak at the funeral?"

"I don't know...I haven't decided. Are you?" Caroline smiled, already knowing the answer.

"Are you crazy?" Tracey's voice got high in pitch. "You know I can't speak in front of anyone."

****

The girls arrived at the funeral home about an hour before the service started. When Caroline first got the phone call about Johnny's death, she had cried for the loss of things he'd

9

never get to do—get married, have kids, or any of that suburban bullshit he probably would have put off for as long as possible anyway. Thoughts of his rebellion made her laugh out loud.

"What are you laughing at?" Tracey asked.

"Nothing. Just thinking." Caroline smiled softly.

"Inappropriate," Tracey informed her with a slight frown.

Caroline's eyebrows raised and her eyes widened. "Right. I forgot how dangerous thinking was. My bad."

"Good thing I'm here to remind you." Tracey nodded.

"Seriously. I'd be some inappropriate rule-breaker without you."

They walked through two large wooden doors into the reception area. The girls noticed Johnny's mom, Jackie, and gave each other a quick, exasperated look. Caroline had always thought Jackie looked glamorous for her age, but seeing her now, in this setting, she stood out like a bottle of vodka at an AA meeting.

Jackie was dressed in a short black mini skirt with a form-fitting, low cut, black top. Her cleavage welcomed anyone who came near. She had on four-inch black heels that accented her ridiculously perfect legs. Her jet-black hair was pulled tightly into a bun, half her face covered by oversized sunglasses. Caroline thought Jackie looked like she was dressed for a night out on the town, not the funeral of her only child.

"Talk about inappropriate," Tracey whispered.

Jackie dabbed at her face with tissue when she recognized the girls. She removed her sunglasses and walked over briskly.

"Tracey! Caroline! Oh…" She broke off into heaving sobs and grabbed the girls tightly, as if attempting to hug the life out of them.

"Hi, Mrs. Lucca. We're so sorry." Caroline spoke through her own tears.

"I know," she lamented. "He loved you girls so much."

"We loved him too," Tracey sobbed.

"Thank you both for coming. Is Clay here?" Jackie asked, peeking over Caroline's shoulder.

"He had to work, but he sends his condolences," Caroline explained.

"Well, make sure to tell him that we missed him."

"I will," she promised.

"Johnny's inside." Jackie nudged the girls toward another set of doors. "You should go see him."

Caroline shot Tracey a brief, uncomfortable look before agreeing. "Okay. So…we'll be back."

"I'm so glad you're both here." Jackie gave them a wan smile and turned toward a small group of adults standing near the guest book.

Tracey and Caroline slowly walked into the parlor where only a few people had gathered. The dark wood walls and lights gave everything a slight orange glow. Johnny's white casket rested at the far end of the room; enormous flower arrangements adorned each side. The girls slowly walked down the aisle toward his lifeless body.

"I don't know if I can do this," Tracey choked out, her face suddenly pale.

"Yes, you can. Come on. Just breathe." Caroline took Tracey by the hand

As they neared the open casket, the girls slowed their pace, finally coming to a stop a foot in front of the casket. Caroline peeked toward his face before they inched closer.

"He looks so weird," she admitted with a whisper. Johnny's face was unusually pale, like a dusty chalkboard, Caroline thought to herself. There was a scratch on his forehead and one on his cheek that they tried to cover up with way too much makeup. In fact, Johnny's entire face was covered in some sort of makeup. A football was tucked under his right arm and the gesture made Caroline smile. She placed a picture of the three of them under his left shoulder and whispered, "We'll always be with you."

"It's so weird not to see him smiling," Tracey noted.

Caroline put her arm around Tracey and took a deep breath. "I know. You know that's not him any more...right, Tray?"

"What do you mean?"

"I just mean, his spirit—or his soul, or whatever you want to call it—it's not inside that body any more. He's probably watching over us right now, laughing or making fun of us," Caroline explained.

"Probably. It still hurts, though." Tracey nodded her head and leaned into her friend's shoulder.

Caroline agreed. "It hurts like hell."

The girls spent another minute in silence before they turned to find seats. The room had quickly filled up behind them and additional mourners stood outside.

Johnny's uncle stood behind a tall dark podium. He spoke through tears about a young life filled with laughter, excitement and adventure. "It's all so fragile. Precious, really. You never think about the fact that it can all be gone in an instant. Hopes and future dreams, all snuffed out."

Caroline watched as he pulled a matchbook from his pants pocket. Slowly, he lit one match and allowed it to burn for a few seconds before a short burst of his breath extinguished the once burning flame. Caroline watched as a single ribbon of smoke billowed up toward the ceiling.

"Johnny was like that match. He brightened every room with his light. And then, just like that," he snapped his

13

fingers, "his light was gone. And all hopes for his future were gone with him."

"Jesus. I'm never going to be able to stop crying now," Caroline whispered into Tracey's ear.

Tracey tried to respond, but couldn't. Caroline grabbed her hand and pulled it onto her leg, holding it tight.

"Caroline Weber would like to say a few words." The preacher's voice broke through Caroline's grief and nerves shot through her.

"Shit," she mumbled under her breath towards Tracey. "Guess I'm speaking after all."

Caroline shakily made her way to the podium sans prepared words, notes, or anything. You gotta wing it, she thought to herself. Standing at the head of the room she scanned the enormous crowd and instantly felt the warmth of love spread inside her. The crowd was a simple reminder to her of how much Johnny had been loved. She couldn't help but smile.

"Hi, everyone. My name is Caroline and I went to college with Johnny. My roommate Tracey, Johnny, and myself were pretty much inseparable. Everyone at school called us the Three Amigos, the Three Musketeers, Three's Company." Caroline rolled her eyes. "People were very creative."

Small bursts of laughter filled the room before Caroline continued. "I can't believe this is happening. It doesn't seem real, you know? I wish it wasn't." Caroline struggled to maintain her composure. "It seems so unfair. I stand here and ask myself, why? Why did this have to happen? Why did it have to happen to Johnny, of all people? Why now? Why, why, why?"

She took a deep breath and wiped at her falling tears. "But there are no answers. There is no reason that would ever be good enough. I will tell you all this though…I'll never be able to look at life the same way again. My perspective has changed. My mindset has shifted. And that's because of Johnny. Even in death, he's still bossing me around."

She laughed and the crowd laughed with her. "Life is too short…and nothing is certain. Nothing. Just because you tell someone you'll talk to them later, or you'll see them tomorrow, there is no guarantee that either of those things will happen. You hope they will. Hell, we all assume they will. But we don't really know. Life can change in an instant. A single instant."

Caroline closed her eyes to blink out tears as she gripped the sides of the podium with both hands. "I'm going to make myself a promise right here and now. In Johnny's honor. I promise to live each day to the fullest. I promise to listen to my heart and then work through my fears to follow it. I promise to realize what my dreams are and then take the steps necessary to make them a reality. I promise to be true to me. Not what someone else wants me to be, but what I want." She glanced at Tracey, who was sobbing.

"Johnny lived that way. And I always envied him for it. He never cared what other people would say. He lived by his heart. He let his passion guide him. He was the best person I've ever known and I miss him so much."

Caroline quickly walked away from the podium and down the steps to her seat. She buried her head in Tracey's shoulder. "That was perfect," Tracey whispered to her.

"Thanks." Caroline's eyes closed as she struggled to hold back her tears.

The preacher stepped behind the microphone to announce, "The burial will take place at plot twenty-three on the East Lawn. It's located right outside the double doors and to your left."

Caroline and Tracey held hands as they crept out one of the back doors. Caroline squinted as the sun momentarily blinded her and fumbled through her purse for her sunglasses. The wind whipped at her hair and she fought to stop it from blowing into her face. She spotted the white casket being carried in the distance. "There it is."

"How do you know for sure?" Tracey asked.

"Look around. There's no one else here."

Tracey scanned the area and noticed that Caroline was right. Aside from the crowd that formed at Johnny's future resting site, the graveyard was empty. They made their way over to the white casket, which was now closed.

The preacher cleared his throat and the girls directed their attention to him. He read a brief prayer aloud before two workers slowly lowered Johnny into the freshly dug ground.

uncomfortable sighs. The woman at the counter knew Caroline's plane left soon, yet nothing sped up her process.

Caroline couldn't stand it any more. "I don't mean to be rude, but my flight is leaving soon and I still have to get through security. I really can't miss it."

The woman stopped instantly, forced a smile and cocked her head to one side. "Dear, we have flights that run all day long. If you miss this one, we'll get you on another."

Caroline fumed. Why did this woman think her time was so invaluable, because she was young? She wanted to reach over the counter, grab the lady by her dark blue vest, and violently shake her. But she knew that was probably a bad idea.

Instead, she lied. "I have meetings all day that I'd really prefer not to reschedule. I'm sure you can understand that, *dear*?" She mimicked the woman's head tilt and half smile.

The woman dropped her smile and her tone turned cold. "Where are you headed?"

"San Francisco," Caroline responded in kind.

"Last name?"

"Weber, with one 'b.'"

"Caroline?" the woman inquired, clearly annoyed.

"The one and only," she smirked.

"I'll need to see some ID."

Caroline handed the woman her driver's license and the woman abruptly handed her a ticket. "Gate A2. Enjoy your flight."

Caroline raced toward security, dreading the ordeal. She placed her black sandals into a bin and made sure her pockets were empty. After a wave from the TSA agent, she walked through the security scanner without a beep. She smiled, grabbed her things in a rush, and sprinted toward her gate.

When she arrived, she was relieved to see her flight was delayed thirty minutes. She headed over to a small restaurant and grabbed a bite to eat before walking back toward the gate. The airline didn't assign seats, but her boarding number assured her that she would be one of the first passengers on the plane. When it was time to board, she walked all the way to the back of the plane and took a window seat.

Caroline listened to music on her iPod and glanced up every so often to see people walk past. As the seats filled up, no one sat in either of the two next to her. She actually started to wonder if she smelled bad or had something on her face. She leaned her nose into her arm and gave a quick sniff. *Definitely do not smell,* she thought to herself.

She almost laughed at her ridiculous behavior, when something internal told her to look up. Her heart raced and she almost choked on her gum when she saw an Adonis walk down the aisle toward her. He was tall, tan, and wore a baseball hat backwards that covered his short, dark brown hair. His deep blue eyes locked onto hers and she was certain her heart stopped beating for a moment.

He couldn't take his eyes off of hers as he walked toward her row. His full lips turned up slightly in a sexy smirk before he said, "Hi," and threw his backpack onto the floor of the aisle seat.

"Hi," was all Caroline could manage in response. He was unbelievably good-looking and she couldn't help but stare. His shirt fit tightly on his chest and his sleeves strained to contain his upper arms. *That's what perfection looks like*, Caroline thought to herself, her lips pursed together.

"Is anyone sitting here?" a teenaged boy asked, interrupting Caroline's mental assessment.

"You," said the hot guy. "But hold your horses, kid," he added as the teenager attempted to squeeze into the middle seat. "I'll scoot over; you take the aisle."

"Are you sure?" the boy asked.

The stranger looked over at Caroline and smiled. "I'm more than sure."

Caroline couldn't help but smile. As the teenager sat in the aisle seat, she tried to sneak a glance at the hot guy who sat next to her. He turned and caught her looking at him and a wide grin crept across his face. Caroline had a weird thing for good teeth and thankfully, his were perfect and bright white. He set fire to feelings she hadn't experienced in years; things she had completely forgotten about when it came to anyone other than Clay.

Clay? At this point, she could barely remember Clay at all.

To be honest, Caroline wasn't sure if she'd ever encountered feelings like this before. She was instantly attracted to Clay because he was so handsome, but this stranger ignited something new inside of her. In a way it was almost primal…she literally felt pulled toward his body. It was as though some invisible cord connected them.

Her body wanted to do things that her mind had to fight off. She stopped herself, more than once, from resting her hand on his thigh, as though that was the most natural place for it to be. She could feel beads of sweat starting to drip down the front of her shirt. He made her nervous and she struggled to stop herself from shaking.

The attraction between them lingered in the air. They looked into each other's eyes for an uncomfortable amount of time before the teenager interrupted.

"Are you two dating?" he asked politely.

Caroline nodded and before she could say a word, her handsome stranger tossed his arm around her and pulled her close. "We are," he answered and then quickly kissed the side of her head.

Caroline's insides were unhinging. What had she gotten herself into? She could pretend she didn't enjoy the fact that his lips had just touched her skin, but that would be a lie. Before she could think another thought, he leaned near her ear and whispered, "I'm sorry about that. I don't know what came over me."

She turned and looked into his eyes. "I didn't mind." Her words made him smile and she couldn't stop the corners of her mouth from turning upright in return.

Caroline fumbled underneath her seat for her purse. When she found it, she pulled it onto her lap. Her new "boyfriend" watched her every move with curious eyes. When she reached inside and pulled out her camera, he smiled in approval. She handed her camera across him to the teenager and asked, "Can you take a picture of us, please?"

Hot Guy scooted his body as close to hers as he could and she felt tiny prickles of energy all around her. It reminded her of when one of her body parts woke up after it had fallen asleep. With her cheek pressed firmly into his, her body buzzed with an unfamiliar feeling, a feeling so foreign and strong, it almost made her jump out of her seat. But the hot guy didn't react at all, so Caroline figured it was all in her head.

"I like it when your face touches mine," he whispered, right before the picture was taken. Her cheeks flushed with warmth.

She thanked the teenager while the stranger looked at the picture and deemed it worthy of keeping. "You look gorgeous. I look like a schmuck," he told her with a scowl.

"Shut up! You look amazing. Your eyes—they're gorgeous." She ran her finger across his face on her camera screen and looked at the blue eyes staring back at her.

He gently took her face in his hands and looked into her soft green eyes. He moved his face toward hers as her heart pounded and her mind felt muddled. He kissed her softly above her ear. "You have beautiful eyes, too."

Heat instantly rushed through every pore of her body. Clumsily, she grabbed her purse and shoved the camera back in before telling him, "Thank you," for the compliment.

"Any time, babe." He winked and she felt lost as she looked at him.

"Excuse me, sir, you have to turn your phone off," the flight attendant told him.

"Yeah, hon, turn off your phone," Caroline smirked. "I'm sorry. He always does this." She rolled her eyes toward the attendant.

He gave her a quick glance and threw his arm around her waist, pulling her into him, "Oh I do, do I?"

His arms were muscular and his chest and shoulders were hard, but Caroline didn't mind. She couldn't remember the last time she was so intensely attracted to someone. Her entire body was aware of his. She briefly thought about Clay, but only to compare the differences between him and her new friend. She told herself to stop touching this stranger, stop flirting, stop doing everything she wouldn't want Clay to be doing. But her body and emotions had their own agenda. And on that agenda was a five-hour meeting with this new, attractive stranger.

When the plane started to take off, she realized immediately how tired she was. She yawned and fought to keep her eyelids from closing when she heard, "Did you want to sleep, babe?"

When he talked to her like they were a couple, she got a rush of jittery emotions. "Maybe just for a little. Don't let me sleep too long, though." She looked up at his seemingly chiseled features before her hand brushed down the side of his face. What was she doing? She didn't know this guy; why the hell did she touch his face like that? This was inappropriate and she knew if Clay were doing this, she'd be livid.

But she couldn't stop herself. Everything about this guy intrigued her. She wanted to be near his body. She wanted to touch him. Her hands wanted to be all over him. She had to fight the urge to kiss him every time she looked in his direction.

He bent down, reached into the black sport bag under the seat, and pulled out a faded gray sweatshirt. He folded it into a loose ball and placed it between his shoulder and her head. Then he gently pulled her body toward his and kissed the top of her head. As he stroked her long blonde hair, she reminded him, "Not too long. Promise me."

"Sure…but why?"

"Because I don't want to waste the whole flight with you sleeping." She nuzzled into his neck and felt his cheek pressed against her head. Unable to keep her eyes open any longer, she stopped fighting the sleep that came for her. Her last waking thoughts were how the sweatshirt pillow smelled just like him and she drifted off while she breathed him in.

Caroline opened her eyes as the jarring movements of airplane turbulence forced her awake. She lifted her head slowly, but kept her arms wrapped around his body. She didn't move her leg, either, which had somehow become intertwined with his.

"You okay?" he asked, without moving. She smiled and the attraction between them was like lightning in the night's sky. He took a quick breath and confessed, "I want to kiss you so bad," as he tucked a long blonde strand of hair behind her ear.

She *wanted* him to do it. Her lips screamed at her to let him. But the reality of her situation, and Clay, was something her conscious mind couldn't get past.

"I...have a boyfriend," she stuttered. It was the truth, but at that moment she wished it wasn't. It was the first time she had spoken those words and felt nothing but disappointment. What was wrong with her? Clay was not the type of guy a girl was disappointed to have.

"I'm truly sorry to hear that. He's one lucky guy," he informed, still holding her.

Caroline's mind drifted to thoughts of kissing this stranger. Touching him. Allowing her hands to roam all over his body. She wondered how bad could it be? She could kiss him and never speak of it again. It was the perfect scenario for a hookup—a plane flight across the country surrounded by strangers. No one would be the wiser. No one would ever know. She sighed softly and thought to herself, *I would know. I could never live with myself if I did that to Clay.*

She inched away from his secure arms and leaned her head into the seat. As they faced each other she said, "I'm so attracted to you. I really want to kiss you, but I can't. It's not right."

"I understand. I respect you for that. But I've still got four hours or so to change your mind," he teased.

"I'll make you a deal. If this plane goes down, I'll let you kiss me the whole way," she told him laughing.

"I've never wanted a plane to crash so badly in my life."

Caroline was keenly aware that this flight would come to an end, this guy would walk out of her life, and she'd be forever changed from it. She felt things stronger than most people. Sometimes she felt it was a curse to feel things so deeply, but other times she felt it was one of her best qualities.

The two of them talked for hours. She kept her legs tangled in his and he acted as if he wouldn't take his arms off of her if someone paid him to.

"So what do you do?" she asked.

He paused for a moment, as if unsure of how his words would sound. "I'm finishing up business school in the city, and I work on my parents' farm."

Her face lit up with surprise. "A farm? In New York? What kind of farm?"

"It's upstate…a dairy farm. We have some orchards, too. I like to help out my dad when I can." He smiled at her and cocked his head in the most charming way.

"You're way too hot to be a farmer," she flirted.

"Oh, really? How many farmers do you know?"

She laughed, then shrugged. "Counting you?"

"Sure. Counting me."

"One." She smiled and her face crinkled up. "Do you like farming? I mean is that what you want to do?"

He laughed at the simplicity of her question. "I do. The farm has been in my family for generations and I want to keep it that way. That's why I'm taking these classes. We have to keep up with the times, you know?"

Caroline warmed, the heat of desire and respect coursing through her veins. "I love how proud you are. And respectful. It's very attractive." He blushed and averted his eyes. She continued to compliment him. "You're smart, passionate, and determined. I really respect that."

He smiled gently. "Thank you." Longing to change the subject he asked, "What about you? What do you do?"

"I'm a marketing assistant for JD Walters," she said proudly.

He cocked his head. "Am I supposed to know who that is?"

She laughed and shook her head. "Not in your line of work. He's one of the best print ad photographers in San Francisco."

"What does that mean? Print ads…like magazines, billboards, and stuff?"

"Exactly. Guess you're not all body and no brains after all," she teased.

"Oh, no no no. I'm definitely all body." He smiled at her.

"My best friend, Bailey, works there too; I've known her since high school. She got me the job, actually."

"You have good friends."

"The best," she smiled.

"Is that where you're from?"

"Where? San Francisco?" Her expression soured. "God, no. I'm from Southern California. I just moved to Nor Cal for work."

"That's…" He paused as he struggled to find the right word. "Convenient."

"I guess so." Caroline smiled. "When's your birthday?"

He cocked an eyebrow at her. "January 17th. Why?"

"Just wondering," she said while her shoulders lifted. "So, what does that make you? A Capricorn?"

He nodded. "I think so. When's your birthday?"

"July 2nd. I'm a Cancer," she informed him.

"Yeah, you are," he responded playfully.

"You're the cancer! You're like a growth or something." She crinkled her nose at him.

He laughed at her cheekiness and mimicked her response before asking. "So why were you in New York?"

"I had to go to a funeral."

"I'm sorry. How did you know someone from New York if you're from California?"

She smiled at his handsome face and stunning blue eyes. "I went to college there. I just moved back to California a few months ago, after graduation."

"Oh. So whose funeral was it?"

"His name was Johnny. He was one of my closest friends. A really good guy…you would have loved him."

"I bet I would have."

Caroline knew he didn't try to be charming, but every word this gorgeous farm boy spoke was nothing but.

"More importantly," she smiled, "he would have approved of you."

He leaned toward her and kissed the top of her head again and the attraction pulsed throughout her veins. She had to fight off the impulse to tilt her head up and allow him to kiss her lips.

Caroline reminded herself constantly that it was wrong. Even though every fiber of her being screamed out for him, she allowed her conscience to win the battle.

"So why are you flying to California?" she wondered out loud.

"I have some meetings for farm stuff, and my buddy is getting married."

"Seriously? So how do you have a friend in California, if you're from New York?" she asked him mockingly.

"He moved out there for work. He loves it. I think he's crazy." He shrugged and smiled.

She laughed out loud. "Have you ever been or is this your first trip?"

"First trip."

"I think you might surprise yourself," she said and winked at him.

"What do you mean?" He leaned toward her, his eyes looking her up and down.

"I'm just saying, you never know. You might love it there."

"Do you?" he fired back in response.

She laughed and told him, "Not at all. But don't get me wrong. I'm from Southern California and Northern is just so different. The weather will be the death of me, I'm sure of it."

"How did you ever survive in New York?" he teased.

"That was different. I tolerated the weather for the atmosphere and the energy. I love it there so much!"

The teenager tried to interrupt their conversation, but Caroline quickly cut him off. "Not now, boy, you're on a time-out."

"For what?" the boy pouted.

"For talking. Quiet time."

Caroline and her stranger laughed as the teenaged boy slumped into his seat and folded his arms with a grunt. Then her stranger leaned in close and whispered, "I wish I could bring you to the wedding."

Having his lips breathe words into her ear sent chills racing all the way down to her toes. She could barely handle it as her heart raced and her breath felt sporadic. "I bet we'd have the best time. Do you dance?"

"Of course," he stated, both confident and sexy.

"Will you think about me?" She played with fire, but thought if he felt the same, then maybe it would make it all less wrong somehow.

"Of course I'll think about you. I've never met anyone like you."

"Well, it's a wedding. Lots of single girls, I'm sure. You'll probably have a slew of new fans before the day is over." She tried to act cool and nonchalant, but deep down she wanted to be the girl who was different—the one who made a guy do things he'd never normally do, behave in ways he'd never behaved, because he met her, or had to have her.

"You're probably right," he joked.

Pangs of disappointment darted through her body as she faked a smile.

The plane started to lose altitude slowly and that could only mean one thing. "I've been dreading that feeling," he confessed, interlocking his fingers with hers.

"What feeling?" she wondered, keenly aware of his touch.

"We're going to be landing soon. I don't want this flight to be over." He rubbed her fingers with his thumb.

She was aware of the moisture that started to fill her eyes and she blinked quickly to keep her emotions at bay. "I don't want to go," she said and then quickly buried her head into his chest.

"Me either," he said, and she knew he meant it.

"I don't want to let go." Caroline refused to unwrap her hands from his body.

He smiled. "I know exactly what you mean."

She felt his grip tighten slightly and she took a slow, deep breath before closing her eyes, completely consumed in him. Her heart hurt and she wondered why and how this stranger could affect her this strongly in such a short amount of time.

"I can't believe this is it." She lost herself for a moment in the blue of his eyes. She stared deeply into them as every thought she didn't dare say aloud floated around in her mind. Like how much she wished she could leave with him. How she wanted to see him again before he left town. How desperately she wanted to kiss those full, gorgeous, soft-looking lips. How she couldn't believe she had to let him go and walk away as though they'd never met.

"I think I'm really going to miss you," he said, his voice half surprised so it came out weird.

She rolled her eyes. "Wow. That was sweet," she said, her voice dripping with teasing sarcasm.

She wanted to grab him by the back of the neck and crush her lips against his. The way his lips moved when he spoke tempted her. Everything tempted her. He leaned close to her face and softly kissed her cheek. The brush of his lips against her cheek made her feel flushed. When he pulled away, the heat still lingered. She struggled to catch her breath.

"And hey," he said softly as he tilted her chin up. "I won't cheat on you this weekend."

"What?" Completely lost in his touch, she had no idea what he meant.

He laughed. "At the wedding. The other girls. Don't worry, babe. None of them will be you."

Her mouth fell open slightly and she didn't respond.

"By the way, this has been the best flight of my life," he confessed to her with a smile, as the plane landed with a few bumps on the runway.

Caroline looked out the small, dirty window at the city in the distance before she turned back to him. "Me too. I can't believe I have to let you walk away." She believed people came into her life for a reason and although she wasn't entirely sure what his purpose was, she knew she had never had feelings like this for a stranger before. She didn't want to let him go, but knew she had to. Letting him go felt wrong somehow, but what other option did she have?

"Bye, you guys," the teenager said, before heading out with the rest of his group. "By the way, you two are a really nice couple."

"Aww, thanks. See ya!" Caroline said to him cheerfully, and then realized they never exchanged names. None of them had.

"Oh my gosh." She looked at her handsome stranger and said, "I don't even know your name!"

"I guess we never really got that far, did we?"

"We kind of skipped all that. I'm Caroline."

He looked at her, his eyes filled with warmth as he extended his hand. "Jax."

"Jax?" she repeated as her lip curled up into a slight grimace.

She thought the name didn't suit him at all until he corrected her. "Jackson."

The grimace quickly turned into a large smile and she nodded her head in approval. "Jackson. I like that."

He tilted his head and smirked with sexy confidence. "I knew you would."

He led the way as they headed out of the plane together and she took in every detail she could about him. He was over six feet tall and his body was incredible. His loose cargo shorts fit him nicely and his shirt couldn't help but hug at the muscles in his shoulders and biceps. She laughed when she saw his sunglasses face her on his backward cap. Out of nowhere, she remembered they took a picture together and she was immediately thankful.

The sign above them read *Baggage Claim* and she knew Clay would be waiting for her there. "Wait," she pleaded, her voice tight.

"What's the matter?" He looked at her with eyes that mirrored her own emotions.

"Just...one last hug." She hated everything about this. Leaving him. Being back in San Francisco. She knew she should feel guilty and her thoughts should be with Clay, but at that moment, nothing and no one else mattered. She had to steal whatever moments she could with Jackson before it all ended. The thought alone made her stomach clench in despair.

Jackson held her tightly against his body and then he kissed the nape of her neck softly. Their breathing was in sync as each rise and fall of their chests matched. Caroline pulled back and looked into his blue eyes before she took a deep breath to steady her nerves. Her eyes quickly turned misty, so she walked away from Jackson, her heart aching with each step.

Clay stood at the base of the escalator with an armful of yellow roses. A smile instantly appeared the moment he saw Caroline coming toward him. She forced a smile in return, her heart longing. As Clay hugged her, she looked over his shoulder and her eyes locked on Jackson's. At that moment, all she wanted to do was break free from Clay and run into Jackson's arms. She knew it had to be written all over her face. She wondered if Clay would be able to tell.

"I missed you. How was the flight?" Clay asked sweetly.

She looked at Jackson and then at Clay, her heart beating loudly in her ears. "It was really nice. I had a great time."

"Really? What made it so great?" Clay asked, his voice piqued with curiosity.

"I just had great conversations and met some really nice people."

Caroline watched as Clay glanced in Jackson's direction and quickly shifted his weight uncomfortably from leg to leg.

"What about him?" he motioned in Jackson's direction.

"Yep! That's who I sat with. He's amazing. Let me introduce you." She pulled Clay reluctantly toward Jackson.

"Jackson…this is my boyfriend, Clay. I just wanted you two to meet." She wasn't sure what the hell she was doing exactly. Why was she introducing them, was she crazy? There's no way Clay wouldn't be able to sense the chemistry between them. Was she signing her own death sentence?

She watched as Clay stuck out his hand and was met with Jackson's much larger one. She noticed Clay wince slightly at Jackson's grip. Clay's eyes narrowed. "Nice to meet you. Thanks for taking care of *my* girl on the flight. She said you were great."

"She's pretty amazing. You're a lucky guy. I'd hold on to her if I were you," Jackson responded confidently.

Caroline freaked, but part of her enjoyed the confrontation. She silently berated herself for liking this sort of thing and then convinced herself that only crazy, insane people would get off on situations like this. The truth was it gave her comfort in the midst of her own internal chaos to know that Jackson was attracted to her.

Clay grabbed her hand tightly and started to walk her out of the airport. He turned to Jackson and said, "It was good to meet you. We have to go...reservations, of course." He sounded snide and condescending. Caroline had never seen this side of Clay before and she wasn't sure she liked it.

"Of course. See you, Caroline." Jackson smiled at her and her heart went into hysterics. She couldn't believe this was it. She walked out of the airport like it was any other flight, when it was anything but. What was she doing? How could she just leave like this? But how could she not? Secretly, she hoped to see Jackson run after her and beg her not to leave with Clay. She imagined the scene like something out of an over-the-top romantic movie where everyone lived happily ever after (of course).

She knew it wasn't right, but at that moment, she didn't care. She felt like she left her heart on the floor of the airport baggage claim. Jackson could either pick it up and carry it with him, or simply leave it there to stop beating altogether. How do you go on living your life as usual, when you feel like that?

"So what did you and Jackson talk about on the flight?" Clay asked her in the car.

"I don't know. Work, life, you. Everything." She was dazed and confused. Her heart was in more pain than it should be in this situation. She stared out the car window, replaying moments that would now only exist in memory. How quickly life turns into pictures…moments captured, quickly lived, forever memorized, or forgotten.

It was then that she realized they hadn't exchanged any information to stay in touch. She didn't even know his last name. They really were never going to see each other or talk to each other again. She did her best to stop the tears, but it was no use. They flowed uncontrollably and her face held so much pain.

"Hey, Care. What's wrong?" Clay's concern only made Caroline feel worse. She didn't cry often, but she had cried so much lately. Whenever she broke down like this, Clay did everything he could to take away her pain.

"Sorry, just overwhelmed from the funeral and everything. I'll be okay." The truth was that not a single one of those tears was for her dead friend. Every teardrop that fell belonged to the one person she was certain she'd never see again. How was she supposed to be okay with that? And why did she feel this way about a person she barely knew?

Caroline grabbed her cell phone and turned it on. "I'm going to text Tracey to let her know I landed," she told Clay with a slight smile.

"Tell her I said *hi*."

Caroline typed a mile a minute. *"Hey girl, just landed. I HAVE to tell you about the guy I met on my flight. I think I'm in love. lol Call you tomorrow."* Caroline pressed *Send* and clutched the phone in her hand.

It took less than a minute for Tracey to reply. *"What GUY? Why do I have to wait until tomorrow? I want to hear NOW, you cheating floozy!!"*

Caroline laughed out loud when she read the text, which caused Clay to ask her what was so funny. She played it off by telling him it was just "girl stuff" and he didn't question her further. *"I can't talk right now…in the car with Clay."* Caroline waited for another response from Tray, but it never came.

Four

It annoyed Jackson how the pit of his stomach twisted as he watched her with him. He berated himself to get over it, but he couldn't shake the feeling that letting her go would be the biggest mistake of his life. Nervous squirming inside his belly urged him to chase after her, but he beat it down. He glanced back at the couple and caught Caroline's green eyes boring into his. The look alone caused his heart to catch.

He watched as Caroline walked out of the airport, Clay's arm possessively around her shoulders, until her blonde hair disappeared from view. His heart burned like wildfire in his chest and he was painfully aware that letting this girl go wasn't going to be easy.

He had never been so taken by a girl before. When he first noticed her sitting alone on the airplane, chills tore through his spine and caused the hairs on the back of his neck to stand on end. He refused to let it show, but nerves uncharacteristically flooded through every bone, every muscle, and every fiber of his being. It almost stopped him from sitting with her, but as he inched closer, her pull grew stronger. Relief greeted him once he sat, followed by an intense longing to close the space between them.

He replayed the introduction with Clay and felt his blood pressure rise. When Clay eyeballed him from head to toe, Jackson ignored the temptation to punch him square in the mouth. He assumed Caroline wouldn't be happy with him if he socked her boyfriend in the face. But did he imagine the sparkle in her eyes when he cautioned Clay to hold onto her? He was certain he'd seen something there. And the guy seemed like a jerk. Sure, maybe Jackson brought out the competitive side of Clay, but his tone of voice and snide comments were uncalled for.

Jackson suddenly felt like a wild animal. He wanted to grab her, steal her, and protect her from anything that could possibly hurt her. But most of all, he wanted to be near her again.

Jackson threw his bags into the back of a cab and gave the driver the name of his hotel. He settled into the back seat and pulled out his cell phone. Alex answered on the second ring. He and Alex had been friends since childhood and Jackson knew he was the right person to talk to about Caroline.

His other best friend, Tommy, was more of a jackass— a typical guy who felt like no girl deserved too much attention. Jackson knew telling Tommy about Caroline meant he'd never hear the end of it. Tommy would never let the fact that Caroline had a boyfriend slide.

"So, did you get her number?" Alex inquired.

"Shit. No. We didn't exchange anything." Jackson leaned his head into his free hand. Before Alex asked, he hadn't realized they didn't give each other any way to keep in touch.

"Really? No email? Nothing?" Alex couldn't understand how they could spend an entire flight together and not exchange any kind of information.

"Shit, Alex. Nothing! This cannot be happening."
Jackson's mind raced. There was no way he was going to just
let this girl walk away and carry on with her life as if they
had never crossed paths. He scanned his mind for all they had
shared on the plane, desperately trying to pick out the one
detail that could bring him to her.

"Maybe it's for the best, man." Alex's tone quieted. "She
does have a boyfriend."

"I know. But it's not like they're married." Jackson knew
he treaded on dangerous ground. His feelings overwhelmed
him, as his thoughts lacked reason. Normally, he'd never
think twice about a girl with a boyfriend. But then again,
he'd never felt this strongly for someone he'd just met
before.

"Jax, did you really just say that?" Alex asked in shock.
"You aren't the home-wrecking type and last time I checked,
you didn't believe in cheating."

"I know. I'm an asshole. It's just…" He paused while he
thought about how to word it. "There's something about
her."

"I think you should just be thankful you two met and call
it a day. If you're supposed to see each other again, then you
will. Can't fight fate."

A light bulb went off in Jackson's head and he shouted
into his cell, "Her job!"

"What?"

"She told me where she worked!" He let out a breath and relaxed back into the cushions of the cab seat.

"Jackson..."

"I know, I know. Dangerous ground, right?" Inside, Jackson knew what he was doing was wrong. But he couldn't fight the way he felt when it came to this girl. The idea of walking away because she had a boyfriend seemed so inconsequential to him. He had to see her again.

"Just be careful. Don't get in over your head. And don't end up getting your ass kicked," Alex warned.

Jackson laughed. "Thanks for the concern. I'll call you tomorrow." Jackson disconnected the call and put away his cell phone. He had a new determination. He scribbled some notes onto a piece of paper and smiled to himself as he watched the city race by.

F i v e

It had been days since the flight and Caroline was going crazy inside. She couldn't stop thinking about Jackson and she searched everything she could think of online to find him. She browsed the dairy farms in upstate New York, just trying to see if one *felt* right to her. But when she found the contact information, there was never a Jackson listed. She searched social networking sites, convinced his name was rare enough to find easily. She was mistaken. Her best friend Bailey tried to talk her into putting an ad online, but Caroline couldn't bring herself to do that.

"Maybe I'm trying too hard? Maybe I'm just supposed to let him go?"

"Maybe, but I don't think so," Bailey offered.

"Caroline, you have a call on line two." The receptionist's announcement boomed from Caroline's speaker phone.

"Thank you, Lisa," Caroline responded politely, assuming it was Clay or a client.

She pushed the button on line two and said, "Caroline Weber." The line was quiet. "Hello?"

"Caroline?" the voice asked. Her heart did backflips inside her chest. She had heard his voice a million times in her head since they parted, but was still shocked at how familiar it was to her.

"Jackson?" The pitch of her voice rose with excitement.

"Yeah. I hope it's okay that I called. It's just that…" He paused, his voice hesitant.

"I'm so glad you called. How did you find me? I've been going crazy, thinking I was never going to talk to you again." She tried to keep her voice quiet since she didn't have a private office at work.

"Do you want to grab lunch? I'd really love to see you."

"Today?" She checked her calendar and looked at her appointments amidst her rising heartbeat.

"If you can."

"I can. One o'clock?" She knew that would give her the most free time between her work meetings.

"Sounds great." He let out his breath with a small whoosh. "Where?"

She mentioned a small restaurant near the wharf and he said he knew where it was. She hung up the phone and cursed herself for her business meeting attire. If she knew she was going to see him, she would have definitely dressed differently.

Bailey stood in her cubicle and looked over the short wall in Caroline's direction. She pointed and motioned her over. Caroline's cheeks reddened with each step.

"Who was that on the phone, missy?" Bailey inquired.

"It was him!" Caroline couldn't hide her excitement.

"Shut up! What did he want? How did he find you? What did he say?"

Caroline laughed at Bailey's questions. "He remembered where I worked. He wants to have lunch. I'm meeting him in twenty minutes."

"Oh, really?" Bailey said with mischief in her voice.

Bailey's expression made Caroline feel conflicted. "Bails, don't look at me like that. You're killing me."

Bailey cocked her eyebrow. "I could always go in your place. Tell him you chickened out. Or grew a conscience or something?"

"Bailey!" Caroline snapped.

"I'm only joking. Have fun...but um, you should probably keep in mind that you already have the world's greatest boyfriend." Bailey winked.

Caroline rolled her eyes at her longtime friend. "I hate you."

"My work here is done," Bailey sassed.

Caroline smiled and turned to grab her purse from her desk. Before heading out, she sent Tracey a text message that said, *"HE FOUND ME!!!! Heading to lunch with him now! Call you later."*

It took less than ten seconds for her phone to ring. "Yes?" Caroline said as she walked out of the office toward the wharf. Tracey's voice was on the other end of the line.

"What the hell are you doing?" Tracey asked accusingly.

Caroline laughed. "What do you mean?"

"I can't believe you're seeing this guy again! Does Clay know?"

"Of course he doesn't know. It's not a big deal, it's just lunch." Caroline tried to downplay the situation.

"If it's no big deal, then why aren't you telling Clay?" Obviously Tracey didn't believe for one second this guy was *no big deal.* Caroline winced.

"You know I can't tell him," Caroline explained, as guilt slowly crept in.

"Because you know it's wrong? You feel guilty? What?" Tracey asked.

For a moment Caroline actually considered calling Jackson to cancel. Then she remembered the promise she'd made during Johnny's funeral. "I do feel guilty," Caroline admitted, "but I *want* to see him. I don't know why, but I do."

Tracey let out a deep sigh. "For the record, I think this is a bad idea."

"Noted," Caroline said sharply. She didn't want to hear this from Tracey. Caroline didn't need help feeling that what she was doing was wrong; she already knew it was. But even her guilt couldn't outweigh her want.

"Don't get mad, Care…I'm just saying." Caroline could tell that Tracey didn't want to fight; she was simply trying to be a good friend.

"I know. Just don't worry. I'll call you later."

With every step Caroline took, her nerves rattled more. What would it be like to see him again? Had she imagined their special connection on the plane? Was he feeling the same way she was?

Lost in thought, she kept walking until her eyes suddenly found his. Seeing him literally stopped her legs from moving. She had imagined his bright blue eyes a million times since she'd left his side that day. But seeing them light up at the sight of her reinforced everything she had been feeling. He looked incredibly sexy waiting for her in his jeans and black T-shirt and she had to stop from running full force into his arms.

She gathered her composure and walked slowly toward him. She threw her arms around his neck and buried her face into his shoulder. All she could think about was how good it felt to be in his arms. Every inch of her body wanted to be touching a part of his. She squeezed him harder and nuzzled into him without any concern for who might be watching.

His arms were wrapped tightly around her waist and his lips brushed the side of her neck before he stopped himself from taking it further.

Caroline didn't want to stop holding him, but the hug had gone long past a simple greeting. She pulled away slowly and looked into his eyes. "Hi," was all she said while she laughed.

He brushed his hand along her cheek like he had done on the plane. She closed her eyes and leaned into his touch. When she finally opened her eyes, he stared at her.

"I can't get enough of you." The words spilled out of his mouth and sent her heart racing. "I'm sorry, I shouldn't have said that." His voice was tinged with guilt.

"It's okay. Don't be sorry." She tried to comfort him. It made her feel less alone to know he felt the same way she did.

"I don't normally do this, you know?" he confessed, and looked toward the ground.

"What do you mean?" she asked.

"I mean, I don't normally go after girls who have boyfriends." His eyes rose to meet hers.

"Well that's good, 'cause I don't normally go after guys other than my boyfriend."

Jackson smiled and pressed on. "No, really. I don't like girls who aren't available. I'm not that guy. I just need you to know that."

"I never thought that about you. And just so you know, I've never been so attracted to another guy since I've been with my boyfriend."

"I believe you," he said sincerely. "I just don't know what to do."

"What do you mean?"

"Nothing," he shrugged as he shook his head.

"Tell me," she pleaded.

"It's better if I don't. Trust me."

"Ooookay," she concurred through squinted eyes.

"God, I love your eyes. They're stunning."

She blushed and quickly closed them. "Oh yeah? What color are they?"

"Seriously?" he laughed. "They're the prettiest green I've ever seen."

"Oh," she stumbled and let out a breathy sigh. "Thanks." She desperately needed to change the subject. "Should we eat?"

"I guess we can't just stand here all day, huh? Food sounds good." He led her into the restaurant and toward the hostess, where he asked for a private table as far away from anyone else as possible. The hostess smiled, looked at Caroline, and scurried off to find something suitable.

"That's okay, right?"

"Of course." She smiled and touched his arm softly.

The hostess returned. "Right this way." She led them to a booth in the far corner of the restaurant. "Is this okay?"

"Perfect. Thank you." Jackson waited for Caroline to sit down before he sat down across from her. They looked at each other in silence for a moment and opened their menus.

"Thanks for meeting me. I really wanted to see you again before I left," Jackson admitted.

"Are you kidding? Jackson, I've been dying inside thinking I was never going to see you or talk to you again. We left without giving each other our cell numbers, emails, or anything. You're all I've been able to think about since I walked out of the airport."

His chest fell as he let go of the breath he held. "Me too. But then I remembered that we talked about work. The first thing I did when I checked into my hotel was look up your work number so I could call you after my meetings."

She reached across the table and gently touched his hand. Waves of emotions coursed through her body. Even her feet started to tingle. "I'm so glad you did." She pulled her hand back. "So, hey! How was the wedding? Did you replace me?" she teased.

He cocked his head to one side and lifted his eyebrows before taunting her, "Wouldn't you like to know?"

She let out a huge, "HA!" before continuing. "Maybe I don't want to know."

He smiled. "It was a really beautiful wedding. But honestly, I kept looking around for you."

She felt her heart THUD inside her chest as her face lost all expression and her jaw dropped open slightly. He quickly apologized. "I'm sorry, Caroline. That was inappropriate. I shouldn't have…"

She cut him off with a wave of her hand. "No. It's okay. I know I shouldn't, but I like hearing that."

"Hearing what?"

"I like hearing the way I make you feel," she admitted.

"Why's that?" Jackson asked, his voice a little shaky.

"Because you make me feel things I've never felt before. I can't explain the way it feels to be around you."

Caroline had never intended to say that much, but it was hard to hold back when he was near. He brought out emotions she found hard to fight off.

Jackson reached across the table and gently stroked her palm with his fingers before admitting, "I feel the same way."

Relief immediately washed over her, quickly followed by an ocean of guilt and concern. What did all of this mean? And what was she going to do about it?

Caroline glanced down at her diamond-encrusted watch, a gift from Clay for their anniversary last year, and noted the time. "I have to go soon. I have a meeting."

"I know," he said. "I mean, not that you have a meeting, but that you have to go."

Caroline felt like she could literally reach into the air and cut pieces of the sadness that lingered within it.

"I don't want to," she admitted.

His eyes were heavy with emotion. "Me neither," he whispered.

They both stood up from the table and walked toward the glass door. This time she practically leapt into his arms, wrapping hers tightly around his neck. Tiny tears spilled onto his shirt. "You're breaking my heart, Caroline. Please don't be sad." He tried to console her as he rubbed his hand along her slender back.

She refused to look at him, so he pulled away gently and lifted her face toward his. He caressed her cheek with his thumb. "Please. No more tears. We'll stay in touch, okay?"

She sniffed and wiped the tears from her face. "Promise?"

"You think I'd be able to leave and never talk to you again? Clearly you have no idea the effect you've had on me, woman."

His words made her laugh. "That's better," Jackson said as he wiped the last tear that remained on her cheek. "God, I want to kiss you." He longed to feel her mouth on his. He had daydreamed about what her lips would feel like, taste like, since meeting her that day.

She debated momentarily between the two questions ever-present in her mind. How much could one kiss really hurt? And could one kiss change her whole life?

Her breath suddenly felt shallow and her knees trembled. "Me too. So bad." She looked toward the ground. "But we can't. I'd never be able to live with myself, or the guilt."

"I know," Jackson agreed. "Why is this so hard?"

Caroline snickered in relief. "I don't know! But it's not normal right? I mean, you don't feel this way about strangers you meet all the time, do you?"

"You know I don't," Jackson insisted.

"So what does it mean?" she asked.

He shrugged his shoulders. "I guess time will tell. You'd better go, babe…your meeting," he reminded her.

"Shit. Well. Keep in touch? God, that's so stupid. This is so stupid," she complained and whined and felt like a jumbled girly mess.

"You'd better go before I refuse to let you."

She recognized the painful longing in Jackson's eyes and knew that her eyes held the same look. The realization that this beautiful, rare thing between two strangers simply had to be let go. She walked away as he stood in the doorway of the café and watched. It was less painful this time, but took more strength.

There she goes again...walking out of my life for the second time this week, Jackson mumbled under his breath.

Her phone beeped and she looked down at the text message notification. *"There has never been a more perfect lunch, or date. Thank you for today."*

She clutched the phone and pressed it against her heart, before typing out a quick response. *"You're the perfect one. Thank you for everything. Have a good flight and text me when you land so I know you're safe. xoxo."*

S i x

Caroline was curled up on the couch eating takeout when her phone rang. She saw that it was Clay and felt the slightest hint of disappointment. She quickly fought the emotion and answered cheerfully, "Hey, babe."

"Hey! I'm leaving the office soon and I just wanted to know if you needed me to grab some dinner?" Caroline usually waited to eat when he got home, but had picked up food on her walk home from the office, her head lost in other thoughts.

"Shoot. I'm already eating. I'm sorry," she said with a guilty conscience.

"No big deal," Clay responded, his voice a little cold.

Caroline noted his tone. "I'm really sorry. I just wasn't thinking."

"It's okay," his tone lightened. "You've been a little *off* since Johnny died. I understand. I'll see you in about a half an hour, okay?"

"'K. See you soon."

When he finally walked through the door carrying a takeout bag from the Chinese restaurant down the street, he took one look at his girlfriend and smiled at her. "What are you smiling at?" she asked saucily.

"My smoking hot girlfriend," he said as he sauntered toward her. He leaned his head down and kissed her passionately, almost falling onto the couch that held her.

When she closed her eyes to kiss her boyfriend of almost two years, all she could see in the darkness of her mind was Jackson's face. No matter how much she tried to concentrate on Clay's kiss, Jackson's image wouldn't fade.

Clay finally stopped kissing her before he looked in her eyes. "I love you."

"I love you, too," she responded automatically, but completely freaked on the inside. Why did she see Jackson's face when she kissed her boyfriend? What kind of girl does that?

"Are you okay?" Clay's head cocked to one side.

Caroline laughed. "I'm fine. Sorry, just lost in thought for a minute."

"What are you thinking about?"

Caroline knew she couldn't tell him the truth. For the first time she could remember, she intentionally lied to Clay. "Nothing. Just work stuff." She desperately wanted to change the subject. "How about you? How was work today?"

She was thankful when Clay took the bait and went on a detailed description about his day. He talked while he ate and she listened intently, while she fought to keep thoughts of Jackson out of her head.

When Clay finished, he threw out his trash and settled in next to her on the couch. It had been a while since he was home early enough to spend time with her, so he promised they could watch whatever *she* wanted on television.

"You'll be sorry," she laughed as she flipped through the channels to find her favorite show.

"Probably," he admitted, "but I don't care."

She laid her head on his stomach and he wrapped his arms around her. Her phone beeped and she shot up to grab it. It was a text message from Jackson. *"Home safe. Flight wasn't the same without you on it. I miss you."* Her heart felt like it beat a million miles a minute.

"Who's that?" Clay asked nonchalantly as he glanced up toward the clock.

Clay's question slammed Caroline back into the real world; for the second time that night, she lied to her boyfriend. "Oh, it's just Bailey."

"Tell her I said *hi*," Clay responded.

Caroline swallowed hard and tried to regain her composure. *"Glad you're safe. I miss you, too."* Caroline needed Jackson to know she couldn't talk to him any further, so she added *"Goodnight"* and pressed *Send*.

After a few minutes passed with no response, Caroline leaned back into the comfort of Clay's arms and lost herself in the television show. Clay ran his fingers through her long hair and kissed the top of her head from time to time. She never moved, pretending to be invested in whatever showed on the screen.

Clay's phone rang and he gently nudged Caroline off of him before taking the call in the spare bedroom of their apartment. It was also their makeshift office and before long he poked his head around the bedroom door and said, "Care, I've got to do some work. I'm really sorry."

She turned toward him and smiled. "Don't be sorry; it's okay."

"You're not upset?" Clay asked, his expression softening.

"Of course not." She shook her head and smiled. "Your work never upsets me."

"Thanks, hon."

The office door closed and Caroline quickly opened up her cell phone to read the text messages from Jackson again. Then she read them one more time. She wanted to text Jackson just to get a response, but turned her phone off instead to curb the temptation.

She wondered how she could feel this way for someone she had just met? She had everything she ever wanted with Clay, so why was she consumed in all things Jackson? She desperately tried to make sense of her feelings. She longed for logic to take over and get her out of this mess, but her emotions wouldn't have any of it. Her heart refused to let Jackson go and she knew she was in for a world of trouble.

****

The next few days were a blur. The only way Caroline could stop thinking about Jackson was to dive completely into her work projects. She stayed late. She got there early. She threw herself into every meeting they would allow.

Her hard work didn't go unnoticed and before long, her internship turned into a promoted staff position. When she got the news she tried to call Clay, but he didn't answer. Caroline hated to leave voicemails, so she hung up. She desperately wanted to tell someone so, without thinking, she dialed Jackson's number.

"Hey, you," Jackson said as he answered.

"I got hired as staff!" Caroline shouted into the phone.

Jackson laughed at her enthusiasm. "Congratulations, babe! That's great!"

"I know! I'm so psyched. I just had to tell you."

"Well, I'm glad you did. Can I call you later?"

Caroline realized that Jackson was in the middle of handling some business and although he didn't want to blow her off, he really needed to go. She smiled at how considerate he was of her feelings.

"I'll call you! Talk to you later," she conceded.

"Okay. Hey, Caroline?" Jackson asked.

"Yeah?"

His voice radiated affection. "I'm proud of you."

Caroline bit her bottom lip with excitement. "Thanks, Jackson. Call you later."

She found more happiness in his reaction than she could have imagined. She realized there would be no getting him out of her head now.

Still beaming from her promotion, Caroline walked through her apartment door that evening and yelled out Clay's name. When only silence greeted her, she took a quick shower, changed into her pajamas, and then snuggled into the couch.

When her cell phone rang she answered it absently. "Hello?"

"Hey, babe. Just calling to let you know I'll be pretty late tonight. Probably won't be home before midnight. You okay?"

"I'm fine. Go back to work," Caroline assured him.

"I love you."

Caroline smiled. "I love you, too."

Once she ended the call with Clay, she calculated the time difference in her head and thought for a second that it was probably too late. It was after eleven p.m. there, but she dialed his number anyway. The phone didn't even ring twice before she heard Jackson's thick, deep, slightly accented voice. "Caroline," he said and chills coursed through her body.

"Hi," she said, half nervous, half confident. Her body wouldn't stop shaking.

"So, how was the rest of your day?" Jackson asked through a crackled reception.

"Amazing! How was yours?"

"Not amazing," he joked. "Hey, are you alone?"

Caroline laughed. "No, my boyfriend's sitting right here."

"Funny. No really, are you at home?" he asked seriously.

Caroline answered, "Yeah, I'm home. Why?"

"Just wondering how you can call me if you're home. Are you hiding in a closet? You are, huh?"

She laughed out loud. "No! I'm in the bathroom!"

"You are, aren't you?" Jackson teased.

"No!" she continued to laugh, "Clay's at work. He's gone most nights until pretty late."

"Ahhhh. That's got to suck."

"I don't mind. I like my alone time," Caroline confided.

"Well, I don't mind that he's gone either."

Caroline heard his voice cut out toward the end. "Jackson? Jackson?" She pulled the phone away from her ear and held it in front of her. The screen read, *"Call Disconnected."*

Before she could redial his number, she got a text message that said, *"Sorry. We get spotty service in our apartment sometimes. Call my home phone."* He included the number and she smiled as she dialed.

"Hello?" A male voice that was clearly not Jackson's answered.

She was caught off guard. "Um, hi! Is Jackson there?" she asked politely, unsure of who was on the other end of the line.

"Depends. Who's this?" the voice asked with attitude.

"Caroline," she informed with equal attitude.

The voice on the other end of the line laughed heartily. "Oh, Caroline! The one from California?" he asked, dragging out the name of her state.

Caroline got excited that whomever she talked to knew who she was. "That would be me."

She heard Jackson and another voice yell in the background, but she couldn't make out what they said. The voice on the phone remarked, "He's not here," and the voices in the background got even louder.

"Oh really?" she asked playfully. "Then why can I hear him yelling in the background?"

"Maybe you're hearing things."

Caroline was confused. Was this guy just playing around with her, or did he intend to be mean? Before she could say anything more the voice said, "You know—Caroline from California—maybe you should be calling your *boyfriend* instead of my friend," and she heard the phone click.

Caroline's jaw dropped in shock as all air ceased to exist within her.

****

"What the hell, man?" Jackson yelled at his roommate.

"You're such a dick," Alex added.

"Whatever. Why is she calling here? What are you doing, Jax?" Tommy chastised his best friend.

"I'm not doing anything. What's your problem?" Jackson yelled.

Tommy shook his head in disgust. "You're being an idiot. Not to mention a complete asshole. She has a boyfriend!"

"We all know she has a boyfriend," Alex chimed in.

"Shut up, Alex." Tommy turned to look at him. "You think this is cool? No big deal that Jackson is talking to someone else's girlfriend?"

Alex shrugged. "I don't know. It's not my business and…it's not like she's married."

Tommy spat out a laugh. "Really, Mister Get-involved-in-everyone-else's-business? Now you see fit to stay out?"

"Enough!" Jackson's voice echoed through their apartment. "She and I are friends. We talk. Now back off."

Jackson grabbed the cordless phone, walked into his room, and slammed the door behind him as he dialed Caroline's number.

"You know this isn't cool, Jackson," Tommy yelled loud enough for him to hear.

"Hello," she answered quietly.

"I am so sorry, Caroline," Jackson told her. She didn't respond right away, but he could hear her breathe.

"Who was that?" she asked.

"That was my roommate, Tommy. I've known him since we were kids. He can be a real jerk," Jackson explained.

"I feel like such an idiot right now," Caroline admitted.

"No, Caroline. Please. It's Tommy. He's the idiot, not you. Don't listen to him," Jackson pleaded. "He's a love-hater."

The phrase "love-hater" coming out of Jackson's mouth made Caroline burst out into laughter. "So, who else do you live with?"

Jackson was thankful she seemed less upset. "Alex. I've known him since I was a kid also."

"Is he a love-hater too?" Caroline asked through her laughter.

Jackson laughed. "Nah. He's a love-lover, for sure."

Caroline continued to laugh and then stopped abruptly. "Oh! I keep meaning to ask you if you have a Facebook page?"

"I don't," Jackson responded.

"Seriously?" she asked with surprise. "Even my parents have them!"

"Well, they are clearly cooler than I am," he laughed. "But it's not really my kind of thing."

"Why not?"

"I guess I'd rather keep in touch with people the old-fashioned way. You know, either in person or on the phone."

"I get it." Caroline sounded disappointed.

Jackson added, "Plus, that site seems to breed a lot of drama. I hear Tommy and Alex talking about it all the time. Who needs that?"

Caroline nodded her head in agreement. "That is totally true."

"You'll just have to settle with talking to me on the phone, through email, and text messages. Think you can handle it?"

"I guess we'll see."

Jackson stifled a yawn.

"Oh sorry. Am I boring you?" Caroline teased.

"Tremendously," he responded. "I hate to say it, but I really need to get some sleep or I'll pay for it in the morning."

"This time difference thing sort of sucks," she moped.

"Goodnight, Caroline. Sweet dreams."

"You too," she whispered softly. "'Night."

Jackson leaned his head into his pillow and as he fell asleep, Caroline consumed his every thought.

****

Caroline hadn't intended to keep in touch with Jackson on a daily basis, but with Clay working most nights, it made talking to him easy. The time difference didn't hurt either. By the time Caroline got in from work, Jackson had long been home, studying or relaxing.

As the days passed, she found herself more and more reliant on Jackson's companionship. When something happened at work, she longed to fill him in. Any news or funny story, he was the first one she wanted to tell. So by the time Clay got home from work, Caroline no longer felt the need to share. When he asked how things were going, he got one-word answers.

"Baby, are you okay?" Clay asked her one night.

Caroline stopped what she was doing and looked in his direction. "I'm fine, why?"

"I don't know. You just seem distracted lately."

Caroline smiled. "I'm sorry. I just have a lot going on at work with the promotion and stuff."

Clay looked confused. "What promotion?"

Caroline scrunched her face in confusion, as well. "Yeah. Since I got hired as staff. You know this."

Clay shook his head. "No. You got hired as staff?" His tone grew in excitement for her. "Baby, that's awesome!"

"I swear I told you," Caroline insisted and thought back to the day she got the news.

"No. I'd remember something like that. So when did it happen?"

Caroline tried to remember when the promotion came through and she thought briefly about lying to Clay, but couldn't. "A few weeks ago."

Clay's face dropped. "Really? A few *weeks* ago?"

"I'm sorry, J...hon. I seriously thought I told you," Caroline apologized.

"It's okay. I've been so busy at work and I'm never around. It's my fault."

"What? Stop it. Clay, it's not your fault. I thought I told you, but obviously I didn't. And that's my fault, not yours." Caroline refused to let Clay take the blame for her idiocy.

He walked over toward the couch and sat down next to her. "Baby, I know I leave you alone a lot. I'm sorry about that. I'll try to be a better boyfriend."

"Oh my gosh, please stop. Are you kidding me? You are not a bad boyfriend. You work hard and I totally understand. I don't care that you're gone. I'm not alone, or lonely or sad or anything. I'm fine. Seriously, I'm the one who's sorry. Forgive me?" Caroline asked sincerely. What kind of girlfriend forgets to tell her own boyfriend something as important as that? The kind who has her priorities all screwed up. Caroline's stomach clenched as the guilt set in again.

"Forgiven." Clay smiled and kissed her lips. "Congratulations on the promotion. You deserve it."

"Thanks, baby," she said, while looking into his hazel eyes.

♡ Seven

Bailey stood inside Caroline's work cubicle and practically shouted, "So you didn't even tell him?"

Caroline shushed her friend and whispered, "I told *Jackson*. But I didn't even tell my own boyfriend."

"Shut.Up." Bailey said, all overly dramatic.

"I'm not kidding. I never freaking told Clay," Caroline continued, "and the worst part…"

"There's a worse part?" Bailey interrupted.

Caroline glared at her. "I *thought* I told him. I didn't even realize I hadn't."

"That *is* a worse part," Bailey agreed.

"And then *he* tried to apologize."

"Of course he did," her eyes rolled.

"This is serious!" Caroline raised her voice in frustration.

Bailey's voice softened somewhat. "Okay. What the hell did he apologize for?"

"For being a bad boyfriend…because he's always working."

"Are you kidding me? What is this guy? A freaking saint?"

"Pretty much." Caroline looked into Bailey's bright blue eyes and asked, "What the hell is wrong with me?"

Bailey laughed and pretended to count on her fingers. "Where should I start?"

Caroline let out a huff. "Bails, seriously. What is wrong with me? What am I doing?"

"Nothing's wrong with you," she responded sternly.

"Then why am I talking to some other guy when I'm currently dating a saint?"

"Maybe sainthood isn't as appealing as it once was."

"Do you think that's it?" Caroline's head spun. Thoughts came at her with warp speed. "No, of course that's not it. I mean, I love Clay."

Bailey put her hands on top of Caroline's and gave them a friendly squeeze. "Maybe it's not enough any more?"

"What are you saying?"

"I'm not saying anything. You are."

Caroline shooed Bailey away and sent a text message to Tracey. *"I need to talk to you. Call me when you have a sec."*

"Having dinner at my mom's tonight. I'll call you when I get in the car."

When her phone finally rang, Caroline took it outside and filled Tracey in on the latest.

"I told you this guy was bad news," Tracey chastised.

"He is *not* bad news. I'm the one who's going around screwing my whole life up."

"Things have gone too far…listen to yourself!"

Caroline held the phone away from her face as Tracey's muffled voice shouted from the receiver. She slowly brought it closer to her ear in time to hear, "How has this one random guy screwed you up this much? I've never heard you act like this—not even when you first met Clay."

"I didn't feel this way about Clay." Caroline's voice shook with guilt.

"What the hell are you talking about?"

"I don't know, Tray. It's just…different," she said, as she stumbled for the right words.

"Well, you have to stop talking to him," Tracey insisted.

"I can't do that," Caroline admitted flatly.

"Can't, or won't?"

"Probably a little of both, I think."

"Do you even love Clay any more?"

The question's brutal honesty stung and Caroline winced. "Of course I love Clay."

"Can you imagine not being with him?" Tracey asked coldly.

A sick feeling washed over Caroline. "Just the idea of that makes me want to throw up."

"Good," Tracey said with relief.

"Good?" Caroline asked, confused.

"Not being with Clay makes you sick to think about…that's a good thing. You love him more than you think you do. Hey, I'm at my mom's. Can I call you later?"

"Of course. Tell Mom I miss her." Caroline thought back to the many times she and Johnny had gone to Tracey's mother's house during college. With the home-cooked meals and the constant fussing, being there felt like being home.

Conflict overwhelmed Caroline's mind as she took a deep breath and headed back into the office. What if Tracey was right?

****

Clay had noticed that since Caroline's return from New York, things hadn't been the same. She was different somehow, distant. He wouldn't have thought much of it if the whole promotion discussion hadn't come up last night.

He wandered the halls of his office when Gina, a pretty brunette who was also an intern, walked up to him. "Can I help you with anything, Clay?"

Clay stopped and looked at her. "Clay?" she repeated.

Clay blinked his eyes a few times. "I'm sorry, Gina. I'm out of it. What did you say?"

Gina flashed a big smile. "I just asked if you needed any help."

"Thanks so much, but I've got it." Clay raised his file folders full of papers up in the air and shook them gently.

"Clay?" she asked, as he turned away. "Are you okay?"

"Yeah, fine. Thanks for asking." He answered with a smile and continued into the copy room.

Gina was a stunner. There was no doubt about that. She had bright eyes and short brown hair that suited her bubbly personality. She reminded him of a pixie. Clay liked how friendly she was with everyone she met. She was also smart and that turned him on, had he allowed himself to be turned on by anyone other than Caroline.

Caroline.

He found himself lost in thoughts of her again. What was it that made Caroline seem so distant lately? At first he thought it was the loss of Johnny, but later sensed there was more to it than that. Night after night he had tried to get close to her, but she often complained about being tired and instead of asking him about his day, she opted for sleep, or her television shows. He could see in her eyes that she no longer lit up when he walked through their apartment door and he couldn't figure out what had made them get so off track. Convinced it was his fault, he wracked his brain for every moment, or piece of a conversation that seemed wrong.

When he couldn't pinpoint it, he got desperate. Desperate for the old Caroline to come back to him…the one who couldn't wait for him to get home from work…the one who talked nonstop about the future. *Their* future. He needed things to be right with her. She balanced him, and if she was out of balance, everything was out of whack. His world made sense as long as Caroline was a part of it.

He hadn't realized it, but he left the office and walked down a busy street. Clay suddenly found himself in front of a jewelry store. His eyes lit up as if they recognized that *"a-ha"* moment that currently stared him in the face. He realized what he needed to do. This would make her happy and everything between them would be right again.

The engagement ring section was the largest in the store. He browsed case after case, peering through the glass at the sparkling diamonds that reflected back at him. He had no idea there were so many styles and types. He almost called it quits right then. Convinced he had to do this, he continued to look at each ring until he found the perfect one. His finger pointed at an almost two-carat princess-cut stone with smaller diamonds on each side. The sales clerk helped him into a back room where they examined the diamonds together and talked over the price.

"This is perfect. I'll take it," he told the saleswoman confidently.

"She'll love it. It's a gorgeous ring."

Clay exited the jewelry store with his new purchase in hand. The green velvet box sat inside a small bag with string handles. His face glowed as he walked toward the office, excited to show off his new purchase. His mind raced with ideas on exactly how and when to propose.

He tried to convince himself he was doing the right thing. It had always been his intention to marry Caroline and he knew she had every intention of marrying him, as well. Sure, this deviated from her five-year plan a little, but would she really mind?

♡ Eight

Bailey bounded in Caroline's direction holding a beautiful bouquet of stark white roses scattered between dozens of bright yellow tulips.

Caroline smiled. "Oh, Bails, you shouldn't have."

Bailey laughed. "I didn't. I saw them delivered and told Lucy I'd bring them over to you."

Caroline grinned from ear to ear. "Clay's never sent me anything other than roses before. These are freaking gorgeous!" she commented excitedly.

"No kidding," Bailey added. Caroline glared at her before Bailey continued, "I mean...no offense, Care, it's just that Clay doesn't really think outside the box, if you know what I mean? He's completely predictable."

"Brat."

Bailey stuck out her tongue. "Just to prove my point...what are your plans tonight with Mr. Matthews?"

"Just dinner that I know of."

"Of course," Bailey said through a yawn.

Frustrated, Caroline exclaimed, "Stop it, Bailey. You like Clay!"

"Of course I like Clay, but he's just so predictable. Sends you roses, takes you to dinner at some fancy restaurant you don't really want to go to in the first place. It's just the same thing all the time. Don't you ever get—I don't know—bored?"

Caroline rolled her eyes. "Not really. I'm not you, ya know. I like knowing what's coming. Knowing what and who I can count on. It doesn't bore me, it's sort of…comforting."

"Boring."

"Secure."

"Whatever you need to tell yourself," Bailey tossed over her shoulder as she walked away.

"Come on. That's not fair," Caroline whisper-shouted at her back.

Bailey stopped and turned back around. "Obviously there is something major going on with this Jackson character. I'm just wondering *why*—if Clay is so perfect and you're so secure and happy—this guy is affecting you so much?"

Caroline's eyes narrowed into angry slits as she spat out, "I don't know."

Before either girl could say another word, Caroline noticed Lucy walking toward them holding a vase that spilled over with dark red roses and baby's breath. The poor girl could barely see around the thing while she navigated through the maze of cubicles.

"These are stunning. Happy birthday, Caroline," Lucy commented, setting the huge vase down carefully onto Caroline's desk.

Bailey and Caroline stared at each other for a moment before either one of them spoke. "Wait. Wait. If the roses are from Clay, then who…?" Bailey dove for the card attached to the tulips before finishing her thought.

Caroline whipped the card out of the flowers and opened it quickly. "Oh my God." The words fell out of her mouth in a whisper.

"What? Who are they from?" Bailey breathed down Caroline's neck while she tried to peek.

Caroline quietly handed the card to Bailey.

"Happy Birthday, Caroline. I wanted to give you a little something that says it all. I hope you like it." There was no signature on the card.

"Jackson?" Bailey inquired.

Caroline nodded.

"Wow. How'd he even know it was your birthday?" Bailey wondered with her hand on one hip.

Caroline struggled to recall their conversations. "I don't know. I didn't tell him." And then it was as though a light bulb went off in her head. Her eyes got wide and she tilted her head back. "Wait. I told him on the airplane. We told each other our birthdays."

"Shut up. On the airplane? That was months ago. You mean to tell me this guy remembered when your birthday was from one mention of it on an airplane flight?" Bailey raised her eyebrows.

"I guess."

"And you're not impressed by that? Hell, I'm impressed by that."

Caroline didn't say a word.

"Well, what did he send you? What's the *little something*" he's talking about on this card?" Bailey demanded.

"I don't know. Do you see anything? 'Cause I don't see any…"

Caroline was cut off by the sound of the receptionist at her desk again. "Caroline, this box was at my desk. I think it fell out of the flowers from Clay. I'm really sorry about that."

"It's okay. Thank you, Lucy."

Bailey looked at her longtime friend. "Well, OPEN IT!" Caroline stared at the small white box in the palm of her hand. It was tied delicately with a simple yellow satin ribbon that matched the tulips.

"If you don't open that box right this second, Caroline Weber, I will!" Bailey threatened.

"Okay, okay. Stop pressuring me!" Caroline slowly removed the top of the box. The first thing she noticed was a business-sized card that read:

"Sometimes When A Heart Is Separated, It Becomes Stronger"

Her heart battered against her ribcage as she carefully removed the card from the box. Under it lay a silver heart charm. It belonged on a necklace, but there was no chain attached. She knew Jackson had purposely left it out. She couldn't wear a necklace with a heart on it that wasn't from her boyfriend.

She removed the charm and looked at every detail. She'd never seen anything like it before. There was a small separation in the top of the heart where the two halves would normally meet. At the bottom, the right half of the heart was slightly longer than the left half. It was the most beautiful thing she'd ever seen.

"Good God, Care. This guy's in love with you," Bailey breathed while she inspected the charm.

Caroline stared at her best friend through tears that began to spill over her eyelashes.

"Oh no, you don't." Bailey grabbed Caroline by the sleeve of her silk blouse and pulled her toward the ladies' restroom. Once inside she peered underneath each stall to make sure they were alone.

"What am I supposed to do?" Caroline implored her best friend for an answer.

Bailey simply hugged her. "What do you want to do?

"I don't know," she cried, her heart at odds with her mind.

"Do you have feelings for him?"

Caroline looked silently into Bailey's blue eyes. It was one thing to know how she felt about Jackson, but keep it buried within herself; it was quite another to admit her feelings to someone else. Once she allowed the words to breathe outside of her lips, she gave them life. She wasn't sure she wanted to give those feelings any more life than they were already taking from her.

"Caroline, come on. Do you have feelings for the guy or what?" Bailey pushed.

"Obviously I do, or I wouldn't be a blubbering idiot in the bathroom right now, would I?" Caroline snapped.

"I knew it," Bailey said smugly. "I just wanted to hear *you* say it."

"Thanks for the support."

"Could be worse." Bailey shrugged.

"Really? How could it be worse?"

"You could be a horrible person that *no one* loved or wanted to date," Bailey teased.

Caroline grinned. "I'll work on it."

Bailey walked over to the paper towel dispenser that hung on the wall and grabbed a single sheet. She turned the left handle on the faucet and placed the towel into the warm running water. Once the towel was thoroughly moist, Bailey turned off the faucet and walked toward Caroline. Black lines of mascara streaked down Caroline's face and Bailey wiped at them, struggling to get them off. "Please tell me you have some makeup here."

Caroline nodded. "In my purse."

"I'll be right back." Bailey rushed out the bathroom door.

Caroline pulled out her cell phone and turned on the screen. She opened her text messages and sent, "*Just got the flowers and the charm. They are equally stunning, thoughtful, and unbelievable. Thank you so much.*"

Before Bailey returned, Caroline's phone vibrated in her hand. She looked down and read, "*Neither are as stunning as you. I hope you have a great day. Happy Birthday.*"

Caroline struggled to catch her breath as Bailey careened through the door. "Jesus, that receptionist is going on and on about Clay's roses. She won't shut up about them. Like she's never seen a freaking rose before."

She went to toss the bright yellow purse at Caroline before she noticed the pained expression on her face. "What happened during the whole minute I was gone?"

"Nothing," Caroline tried to lie.

"Don't bullshit me, or I'll take the makeup back." Bailey tucked the purse tightly under her arm.

"Nothing. Really. I just sent Jackson a text and he responded."

Bailey held out her hand. "Gimme your phone."

Caroline didn't move.

Bailey folded her arms across her chest. "Fine, then. Read it to me."

Caroline grimaced before opening up the text message and reading it out loud. She watched Bailey's expression change to disbelief with each word.

Bailey fanned Caroline's face with her hands in a vain attempt to get it to return to its normal color, instead of the beet red that spread over her cheeks. "You have to calm down, Care, or we'll never get out of here. And I am NOT trying to spend the rest of my life in some old bathroom."

"I'm trying. I'm so sorry." Caroline's eyes began to fill again.

Bailey snapped, "NO! I cannot fix your mascara again. No tears! Think of clowns, or unicorns, or something else happy!"

Caroline placed her palms against her forehead and concentrated on breathing slowly and methodically.

"Not to add more pressure or anything, but your situation doesn't really seem to be getting any better."

"Trust me; I've noticed." Caroline took another long breath to steady her pulse.

"Seriously, Care, I'm sorta worried about you."

"I'm sorta worried about me too," Caroline admitted. "I don't know what I'd do without you."

"Your life would suck…obviously." Bailey's voice softened. "Are you feeling better?"

Caroline nodded.

"Good. But you still look like shit, just so you know."

Caroline eyeballed her reflection in the mirror. "No, I don't."

Bailey smiled. "Nah, you don't. Can we please get out of here now?"

"After you," Caroline gestured.

♡ Nine

Clay arrived home from work right on time, as promised. Regardless of what Bailey had said earlier, Caroline appreciated the fact that Clay made a big deal out of special occasions. Knowing they'd go somewhere nice for dinner, Caroline slipped into a tan fitted dress that stopped short of her knees. It had barely-there sleeves and a scoop neckline. The dress hugged her body in all the right places and accented her thin waist and gentle curves. She wore black strappy sandals that made her long legs look even longer. Her lengthy blond hair was tossed on top of her head in a sexy and attractive up-do. Random strands of blonde hung down around her face.

Clay's jaw dropped when he saw her. "Wow. You look amazing." He walked over to her, took her hand in his and kissed it. "Happy birthday." Then he cupped her face and softly kissed her on the mouth.

She smiled; his kiss felt comfortable and familiar. "Thank you."

"Let me change real quick and I'll be right out," Clay promised, and ran toward their bedroom.

Caroline looked into the full-length mirror one last time before she rolled her eyes at her reflection. Sometimes she simply hated getting all dressed up and eating at fancy restaurants. Everyone always seemed so stuffy and boring. She would much prefer going somewhere simple, but she'd never tell that to Clay. She knew how much he enjoyed taking her out to do expensive things. He associated expensive with nice and he always wanted to do nice things for Caroline. She appreciated his thoughtfulness, but sometimes wished he were a little more in tune with her wants.

When she realized what she thought, she quickly chastised herself for being ungrateful. Then she reminded herself that everything Clay did for her came from a good place.

He walked out wearing a freshly pressed light gray suit. He had on a white button-down shirt with a blue tie. His dark hair was messy, just the way she liked, and the image of the first time she ever saw him flashed into her mind.

Caroline couldn't help but smile at how handsome her boyfriend was. "Talk about amazing."

His smile was genuine and he gave her a quick kiss before he led her out the door by the hand.

"So, where are we going?" Caroline asked, knowing full well he wouldn't tell her.

"You'll see," Clay teased.

"Do I get a hint?" Caroline pleaded.

"Nope," Clay answered, giving nothing away.

Caroline let out an audible gasp as they pulled into a gravel parking lot that overlooked the ocean. Clay slowed the car to a stop as the crunch of the rocks underneath the tires cracked and popped. The chill of the night's air forced Caroline to wince briefly before Clay quickly wrapped his arm around her and tucked her tightly against his side.

"It's freezing," she noted.

"I'll keep you warm."

They walked quickly toward the white three-story building as Caroline's eyes sparkled with delight.

"I've never seen so many windows in a restaurant before. It looks like it's from another time. It's gorgeous."

"Wait 'til you see the inside."

Caroline smiled, marveling at the architecture that appeared almost museum-like. White marble columns and windows that stretched from floor to ceiling adorned the entire structure. Clay held open the oversized glass door and ushered Caroline into the warm lobby where she let out a sigh of relief.

"Wow." Caroline looked at black and white photos of the restaurant in all of its incarnations framed along the wall. "Oh my gosh, did you know it survived the earthquake and the fires of 1906 only to burn down a year later?" She looked at Clay, a mixture of shock and sadness in her eyes.

He smiled and nodded his head as he gave the hostess his name.

"And then they rebuilt it two years later…but it's changed five times since then!" She traced the outline of the building from 1909 with her fingers, entranced by its elegance. Then she looked at Clay and added, "I'm glad they restored it. Did you see these other buildings? No charm or magic at all."

"I agree." Clay sweetly took her by the hand and followed behind the well-dressed hostess.

"The outside sort of reminds me of the Getty Center back home. You know, the old one in Malibu, not the new one."

Clay's face lit up. "You're totally right. It does."

"Will this be okay, Mr. Matthews?" the petite hostess asked softly, not wanting to interrupt the other diners.

Clay surveyed the corner table with its panoramic ocean views and replied, "It's perfect. Thank you."

Caroline immediately looked through the glass and noted small lights illuminating the outdoor balcony and pathway down to the water.

"I'll never get used to all these rocks," Caroline said as her mind drifted to the sandy beaches back home.

Clay's brows knitted in confusion momentarily before they relaxed. "Oh, in the water you mean. It's weird, right?"

"It's just different. We don't have giant boulders jutting out of the water at home. I mean, look! They're all over the place. How does anyone surf here?" she laughed.

"Good question." Clay responded, his voice shaking.

"Are you okay?" Caroline asked, overly aware that his responses were short and somewhat odd for him.

"Of course. I'm just a little tired is all. You okay?"

She grinned with sincerity. "I'm fine." She stared out the window and watched as the water crashed onto the giant boulders, sending parts of the sea hurling in all directions. She thought how the water seemed angrier up here than it did at home. In Southern California, the ocean lapped at the sand. It rolled softly onto the beach and then lulled itself back out again. It never appeared mad or angry, the way the ocean waters seemed to up here.

"Do you remember when we first met?" Clay asked and interrupted her mental comparison.

"Of course I do." Her eyes softened at the memory.

"My little social butterfly." Clay reached across the table for her hand.

"My little wallflower," she responded with a laugh.

"Good evening," a voice boomed between them. "I'm Becky and I'll be your waitress tonight." Her smile was big and her teeth, a perfect shade of white. Her long black hair was pulled into a slick ponytail that accented her cheekbones. She wore a white button-down shirt and black slacks. Caroline noticed that she wore a black bowtie as well and thought to herself how cute it looked.

Becky gently placed a small wicker basket in the center of the table before asking, "Can I start you off with something to drink?" She looked from Caroline then back to Clay.

Clay looked at Caroline. "Care, would you like some wine?"

Caroline took a quick breath. She hadn't even looked at the wine menu yet. "Um, sure. Do you have any recommendations? I like the sweet stuff," Caroline said with a chuckle.

Becky smiled and her large hazel eyes seemed to smile as well. "We have a really nice Riesling or a Gewürztraminer. They're both really sweet."

"Which one do you prefer?" Caroline wondered.

"Um, personally, I like the Gewürztraminer the best."

Caroline eyed Clay who nodded his head in approval. "Okay. Let's do that," she chirped.

"Would you like a glass or a bottle?"

"We'll take a bottle, thanks," Clay answered.

"Great, I'll be right back." Becky turned to walk toward the large oak bar.

"Happy birthday, baby." Clay looked longingly into her eyes and Caroline felt herself get uncomfortable as thoughts of Jackson invaded her mind with a vengeance. She struggled to fight them off.

"Thanks, babe."

Caroline peeled back the forest green cloth napkin in the basket and revealed a small loaf of fresh bread. The warmth rose briskly to her fingertips and she pulled her hand back.

"Ah, that's hot," she waved her fingers back and forth.

"I'll get it for you." Clay gestured politely as he tore a chunk from the loaf and placed it on a small plate. "Here you go, baby." He scooted the plate toward her.

"Thank you." Caroline reached for the glass that held olive oil and poured a small amount onto her plate. "This is cute," she said, referencing the hand painted olives and sunflowers that adorned the bottle.

Becky quickly returned with the wine and two glasses. She placed a glass in front of each of them and proceeded to pour a small amount of wine into each one. Clay swirled the wine around in the glass and then sniffed it before trying the sample.

Caroline grabbed her glass and took a sip. "It's so sweet. I love it!"

Becky stifled a laugh and turned her attention toward Clay, who smiled at his girlfriend. "It's good, thanks."

Becky filled their glasses. "Are you ready to order or would you like a few more minutes?"

Clay eyeballed Caroline. "I'm ready if you are."

Caroline nodded before ordering the seafood and pasta special. Clay waited until she handed the waitress her menu and then ordered some sort of fish dish that made Caroline laugh.

She looked up, her cheeks flushed with embarrassment. "Sorry, that's just a funny name."

Once Becky turned her back, Clay grabbed his wine glass and lifted it from the white linen tabletop. "Happy birthday, Caroline. I love you." He smiled before glancing upward. "And cheers to you, Johnny. We miss you, brother. Wish you were here."

Caroline felt her chest deflate. "To Johnny. I miss you so much." She tried to focus on her smile, but felt the moisture rushing to her eyes.

"I'm so sorry. I didn't mean to make you sad." Clay reached for her hand across the table.

"It's okay. It was a really sweet gesture."

"Know what you want for dessert?" Clay changed the subject, his voice bright.

Caroline knew he was desperate for her to be happy on today of all days, so she went along. "I didn't even look at the menu yet, but definitely something chocolate-y!" Her mind bounced around from thoughts of Johnny to thoughts of Jackson; two people who brought pain to her heart for vastly different reasons.

"Chocolate it is, then," Clay agreed.

When dinner was over and Caroline had convinced Clay she couldn't eat another bite of their chocolate lava cake dessert, he stood from the table and helped her to her feet.

"I think that was the best meal of my life," Caroline commented. "Thank you so much for dinner, Clay. This place is beautiful."

He kissed the top of her hand. "You're welcome. Happy birthday."

As they walked hand in hand toward the exit of the restaurant, Clay started to reposition the jacket he was holding. "Here, take my jacket," he said as he wrapped his suit jacket around her shoulders. "I want to show you one more thing."

"What is it?" Caroline asked, intrigued.

Clay walked her toward the cliff edge of the restaurant as the sound of water crashing filled her ears. She listened to the ocean ebb and flow with harsh intensity and marveled at how much peace it brought her senses.

Clay stopped at the balcony that overlooked the bluff and held her in the warmth of his arms.

"You know how much I love you, don't you?" he whispered into her ear.

Caroline turned to face him. "Of course I do," she told him convincingly, completely unaware of his intentions.

Suddenly, Clay dropped down to one knee, and Caroline's stomach turned with equal parts excitement and fear. He held open a dark box; even in the moonlight Caroline saw the contents sparkle wildly. He spoke words she barely heard over the sound of her own heart pounding in her ears.

"Caroline Weber, will you make me the happiest man alive and do me the honor of being my wife?" She heard those last words loud and clear before the silence that followed.

She was shocked and caught off guard. Then disbelief, happiness, sadness, excitement, fear, and elation dashed through her very being. Her mind raced through what felt like a million thoughts and questions simultaneously.

He wasn't supposed to be proposing already. It was too soon. She wasn't ready. Did Clay really want to marry her? She didn't deserve him. She was lucky to have him. Was this even what she wanted? How could this amazing guy want to spend the rest of his life with her? Was he crazy? She was definitely crazy.

And then guilt crept inside her mind, quickly followed by images of Jackson.

Jackson.

The thought of him almost stopped her heart completely. Her knees started to shake forcefully and she reached for the cold iron railing, bracing herself against it. Another thought of Jackson caused her stomach to lurch violently and she briefly contemplated the notion that she might actually get sick right there on that balcony.

How had she come so far from where she had always intended to be, which was right here, in this moment with Clay? She knew she couldn't possibly tell him 'no.' How could she? Oh sorry, honey, but I've been talking to some other guy and I think I might really like him? Of course she had to say 'yes.' What other choice was there?

It seemed as though minutes passed in Caroline's hesitation to answer, but they were mere seconds in reality. She looked down at her boyfriend, who looked uncomfortable being on one knee, and told him with a smile, "Of course I'll marry you."

Clay's eyes lit up as he gently slipped the diamond ring onto her finger. Caroline marveled at how large the square diamond looked on her hand. She immediately understood why women fell in love with them. "So sparkly," she said out loud, transfixed by its shine.

Clay hesitated and then asked, "Do you like it?"

"It's unbelievable," Caroline admitted, her eyes still glued to her left hand.

Clay picked Caroline up in his arms, breaking her gaze. No longer bewitched by its sparkle her mind quickly returned to the image of Jackson's face. Unable to fight her emotions any longer she allowed the tears to spill out.

Clay kissed the side of her wet face and repeated, "I love you so much."

"I love you too," she told him, as her heart sank.

♡ Ten

Jackson looked down at his phone and felt his heart race as he saw Caroline's name flash across the screen. He pushed the *Talk* button and said, "It's stupid how happy it makes me to see your name on my phone."

She laughed slightly. "Hey, Jackson." Her tone of voice was apprehensive and he knew immediately that something was wrong.

His heart raced wilder now and his stomach felt like it had dropped to his feet. "What's up?"

The pause between his question and her answer made his brow start to bead with sweat. He breathed quicker as he heard her blurt out, "Clay asked me to marry him last night."

Jackson leaned the back of his head against the wall harder than he had intended. He took a long, deep breath. "Well, what did you say?"

She didn't respond and the silence between them made Jackson nervous. His voice shook when he asked her again, "Caroline. What'd you say?"

He heard nothing except the sound of her breath in his ear. He slammed his free fist into the floor beside him and shouted, "Caroline!"

His voice broke as he pleaded one last time, "Oh, Caroline, what did you say?"

He heard her swallow hard. "I said yes."

Jackson blocked out the sound of her tears as his heart felt like it stopped working and he struggled to catch air. His shock quickly turned to anger as he slammed his head against the wall one last time with such force that it knocked a picture down. It crashed down violently a few feet from where he sat, but he didn't move an inch. "I have to go."

"Jackson wait! I only…" He hung up before she finished.

Dazed and heartbroken, Jackson walked somberly into the living room. He grabbed an old record and slid it from its protective white paper wrapping. Gently, he placed it on the now antique record player his grandfather used to own. He watched the record spin for a moment, fascinated by the way the needle of the player bobbed up and down with the grooves of the track.

Then he walked into the kitchen, grabbed a shot glass out of the cabinet and a bottle of tequila. Jackson rarely drank to the point of getting drunk, but tonight—there would be no stopping him.

Jackson lost himself in the old records, appreciating the music and songwriting of the past. Lyrics about heartbreak spilled from the speakers and Jackson did little to stop the tears. The picture of him and Caroline from the flight that day sat on top of the wood, a glaring reminder of what he'd just officially lost.

"How could you?" he asked the picture. "You can't want to marry him. You just can't." He poured the amber liquid into the tiny glass repeatedly, wincing with each one he threw down his throat. He rested his head on his forearms and let the tears spill out around him.

Just then, his roommate Alex walked through the door. He heard the song blaring while outside and knew something was wrong. He saw Jackson sitting at the table, his head buried.

"Parks?" Alex said, calling Jackson by his last name. "Man, you okay? What's going on?" Alex walked toward the table and leaned against a chair.

Jackson looked up from the table slowly. His eyes were beet red and his face was flushed. Pieces of dark hair appeared to be glued to his forehead. He poured another amber shot and chugged it without saying a word.

"Enough with the tequila." Alex grabbed the bottle, glanced at how much was gone and quickly put it back in the cupboard. "What happened, man? Talk to me."

Alex watched Jackson stare at the picture of him and Caroline, refusing to look away from the green eyes that looked back at him. Jackson rubbed her image with his thumb and started to tighten his fist. Just as quickly as the photo had started to ball up, he slammed it down against the flat table top and pressed his palm across it to smooth it back out.

Alex left the room and Jackson overheard him on the phone.

"He's playing a record," Alex said.

"Shit. Really?" Tommy asked.

"Really," Alex said in a matter-of-fact tone.

"What the hell happened?" Tommy knew Jackson only put his grandfather's old record player to use when he reminisced about the past or when he was destroyed emotionally. The only other times he remembered it playing was when Jackson got the news that his grandfather had died, the day of the funeral, and when he missed the old man so much it hurt.

"I have no idea. He won't talk," Alex said.

"I'll be right there. Shit." Tommy hung up and Alex headed back into the kitchen.

"Tommy's on his way. You wanna tell me what's going on?" By now Alex knew it had something to do with Caroline. Jackson knew Alex supported his feelings about her and had sincerely thought they would end up together. He had told Jackson on more than one occasion that he hoped it would work out between them.

Jackson looked up at his friend. He wiped at his eyes, but refused to speak. The truth was, he didn't want to have to tell this story more than once, so he silently waited for Tommy's arrival.

Tommy barged through the door, took one look at Jackson and asked harshly, "What the hell happened? You look like shit."

"Asshole," Alex barked.

Jackson looked down at the table and tried to control his emotions. He didn't want to cry in front of his friends, but this was too much. He eyed his friends and choked the words out, "She's getting married."

"We're going out." Tommy walked over to the record player and turned it off. He grabbed a coat for Jackson and his keys.

Jackson attempted to protest, but it was no use. "We're going out. You're not going to sit here miserable, listening to Otis Redding all night. Let's go."

Jackson begrudgingly walked out of the apartment door, sat alone in the back of Tommy's car, and stared out the window. He knew exactly where they were headed.

The bar was filled with people and a crowd of familiar faces was the last thing Jackson wanted. He marched straight to a booth in the far back corner of the darkened bar. Jackson slid into the side that kept his back to the crowd while Tommy and Alex sat across from him.

"Sally, can we get a pitcher here?" Tommy shouted at the slender bartender from their booth.

"So, when did it happen?" Alex asked.

"I guess he asked her last night. Happy birthday to her, right? I just can't believe she said 'yes.'"

Tommy shook his head, disgust evident in his eyes and the grimness of his mouth. "What do you mean you can't believe she said 'yes?' Of course, she said 'yes.' What was she supposed to say? 'Sorry, sweetheart, but I'm in love with that dude from the airplane?'"

Jackson's stomach dropped as he tried to stop everything inside him from falling apart. He wanted to get angry; Tommy had been telling him for months now that this was a bad idea, but Jackson had refused to listen. Convinced that Tommy was a cynic and couldn't possibly know what he and Caroline shared, he told himself over and over that Tommy was wrong.

"Why you gotta be like that?" Alex chastised Tommy, as the bartender put a pitcher down on their table with an extra frosted glass.

"You okay, Jax?" she asked, noticing the color and puffiness around his eyes.

"Yeah, I'm good. Thanks, Sal." He tried to smile at her so she'd leave.

"All right, let me know if you boys need anything else. And Tommy, you don't gotta holler at me like I'm some sort of cattle or something."

"Sorry, Sally." Tommy winked and reached to playfully smack her behind, but she scooted away. "So, what are you going to do?"

Jackson looked at his two best friends and shrugged his shoulders.

"Well, what you ought to do is…" Tommy turned to look in Sally's direction and gave his head a quick nod, "you know…Sally."

"Not this again…" Alex shook his head while Jackson peered over his shoulder at the attractive brunette. She glanced up and Jackson quickly turned away from her sympathetic gaze.

"What? I'm just sayin'. She's only had a crush on you since we were kids."

Jackson buried his head behind his hands. "Sally's great, but I've never really thought of her in that way before."

"Well, maybe you should start. She's hot. And you're an idiot," Tommy added.

"Enough. I don't want to talk about this any more." Jackson rubbed at his eyes and temples.

Tommy raised his eyebrows with disapproval. "Whatever. So, are you going to fly out to California and kidnap this broad, or what?"

Jackson's chest puffed out before he let out a long sigh. "No. I'm going to walk away."

"Smartest thing you've said since meeting her," Tommy commented and leaned into the tall backrest.

Jackson winced. It wouldn't take much to break him. He was so broken already.

Shock instantly covered Alex's face. "What? Don't listen to Tommy. Have you even told her you love her?"

"Does it matter?" Tommy asked.

"Of course it matters! How can you be pissed at her, if she doesn't even know how you feel?" Alex asked logically.

"I hung up on her before she could tell me anything else," Jackson admitted, his gaze falling to the floor.

"You're a charmer," Tommy choked out.

Jackson quickly looked up and shot his buddy a nasty look. "Shut up and pour the beer."

Alex chimed in quickly, "I'm just going to say this one time, okay?"

"Here we go." Tommy rolled his eyes. "Dr. Phil to the rescue."

Alex gave Tommy a quick punch in the arm. "You have to lay it all on the line. You can't expect the girl to ruin her life for you if she doesn't even know how you feel about her."

Jackson peered up from behind his beer glass and then continued chugging it.

"I mean it, Jackson. You want her to leave her boyfriend..."

Tommy interjected, "Ahem! *Fiancé!*"

Alex continued, "My bad. You want her to leave her... *fiancé...*"

"Thank you." Tommy tipped his head and lifted his glass in the air.

"But for what? For some guy who hasn't even admitted what he really feels for her? She doesn't even know you love her. She probably thinks you don't. No girl in her right mind would leave what she has for that."

A subtle spark of light flickered from deep inside Jackson's eyes. "You're right."

"Of course I'm right." Alex smiled. "And by the way, everyone knows you're a good guy. You'd never intentionally hurt anyone. You're not the girl-stealing type. I know it goes against everything you believe in to be in this type of situation, but you have to give your pride a rest and listen to your heart, or you'll regret it."

Tommy rolled his eyes. "Jesus, Alex, are you really a girl? Do you have a vagina?"

"You're such a dick," Jackson commented half-heartedly.

"At least I have one," Tommy bit off in response.

Alex interjected. "My point is...would you be okay with losing this girl forever?"

Just hearing those words made Jackson want to beat the living shit out of every guy in that bar. It also made his knees want to buckle and his stomach turn inside out. He couldn't answer Alex, so he simply shook his head and lost himself in the pattern of wood on the table.

"Then you have to tell her how you feel...give her all the information she needs...that's the right thing to do. Expecting her to make life-changing decisions based on how only she feels isn't fair, especially when she doesn't know that you feel the same way." Alex glanced down toward his friend who refused to look up.

Jackson swallowed the last of his beer and asked, "Are you done?"

Alex laughed. "Yeah, I'm done."

"Good." All Jackson could think about was how much physical pain he was in, and how much beer it would take to numb it. "Someone get another pitcher."

♡ Eleven

Caroline felt ill. If you'd asked her a year ago what she wanted out of life, this was definitely part of the plan. She had always felt that Clay was the one.

That is, until she met Jackson.

Now everything was wrong. It all felt out of place. She struggled with her feelings and desperately tried to sort them out, but nothing seemed logical. Everything was a huge mess. Were her feelings for Jackson real, or were they fabricated, at best? She didn't know for sure.

After a quick call to a *not so surprised about all the drama, but was still sorry it was happening* Tracey, Caroline called Bailey who said, "Get over here and stay with me tonight."

Caroline knocked on Bailey's apartment door and her shoulders dropped in relief at the sight of Bailey's sympathetic face. Bailey grabbed her in her arms and that was all Caroline needed to start the waterworks.

She tossed her purse onto the faded blue couch and leaned against the wall. Then she fell apart. She could barely speak through her sobs and when she did, Bailey could hardly understand what she tried to say. "So you're saying that you told Jackson about the proposal?"

Caroline nodded.

"Oh, God, Care. Did he freak?"

Caroline nodded again and Bailey walked to the kitchen and poured a tall glass of water.

"Here, Care, you've got to calm down. Please. Take some deep breaths and then let's talk about this." Bailey sat against the wall next to her crying friend.

"O…o…" But all Caroline could do was cry and try to breathe. "O…okay." She tried desperately to stop the tears that fell. "He's so angry, Bailey. He's so mad at me."

Bailey rubbed her hand along the length of Caroline's back. "Of course he's angry. He's devastated."

"What do you mean?" Caroline looked at her with tear-filled eyes.

Bailey chuckled. "What do you mean, *what do I mean*? Stop being stupid. He loves you. He doesn't want you to marry someone else. Can't you see that? You have to know that. I mean, reverse the situation—how would *you* feel?"

Caroline sat for a moment and allowed her mind to do exactly that. Now it was Jackson who had the girlfriend. And Jackson who delivered the news that he was engaged. She immediately felt nauseous at the made-up thoughts and reached for the empty trash can nearby.

"Oh no, you don't. No emotional puking on my watch, missy." Bailey snatched away the blue canister and handed her the water instead.

"How do you know he loves me?"

"Are you really that naïve?" Caroline flashed a look through angry eyes, which only made Bailey grin. "He's a *GUY,* Caroline…a guy who is getting nothing from you. I mean, no loving, no nookie, no nothing!"

Bailey cocked her eyebrows and threw a hand in the air. When it was clear that Caroline still didn't understand, she continued. "Ugh. He still texts you, emails you…spends hours on the phone with you. He goes out of his way to spend time with you and pay attention to you. Guys don't do that—especially when they're not getting anything physical in return—unless they care about you."

The words sent Caroline into a tailspin of emotions. Shooting pains ricocheted through her chest. "What do I do? I'm such a mess, Bailey. What do I do?"

Bailey looked at her friend. "I can't tell you that. Look, I know you love Clay. And I know that Clay is a really great guy."

Caroline nodded her head in agreement. "So you think I should stay with Clay?"

"I didn't say that. I just said I know you love him and I know he's great. And I think you guys could be perfectly happy together." Caroline acknowledged Bailey's words with a knowing look.

"But I also know that in all the years I've known you, I've never heard you talk about any guy, *ever,* the way you talk about Jackson," Bailey continued. "And I've never seen you light up the way you do when it comes to him."

Bailey paused for a moment. "I also know that you wouldn't be doing this for just any guy. I think if you could make your heart stop feeling things for Jackson, you would because you think that's the right thing to do. You never want to hurt people and you always want to do the right thing. I think people come into our lives for a reason, Care. For whatever reason, Jackson came into yours…but for a completely different one, he hasn't left. And you haven't let him. So you tell me."

Caroline answered, "I know what I want. Like, I know what my heart wants me to do. I know where I want to be. And it's not here. It's not with Clay. And just saying that out loud makes me feel like a terrible, awful person. Everything about this situation seems so wrong…hurting Clay…breaking off the engagement. That doesn't feel good. Why should being with Jackson be this difficult? If we're really supposed to be together, wouldn't it be easier?"

"Are you kidding? Who made that rule 'cause I'd love to give them a piece of my mind," Bailey sassed.

"I don't know that I can do it."

"Do what exactly?" Bailey pressed.

Caroline eyed her. "I love Clay. I really do."

"No one doubts your love for Clay."

"But what if leaving him is the wrong choice?"

"No one said you have to leave."

"Am I being stupid, though? I mean, realistically, I barely even know Jackson. It's wrong to leave my boyfriend for someone I don't really know, isn't it?"

"Are you leaving Clay for Jackson?" Bailey inquired.

"No." Caroline looked at the floor, tears spilling all around her. "But if I did, everyone would hate me. Good people don't do things like this. They'd all get shirts that said 'Team Clay' or something."

Bailey couldn't stop from laughing. "I'd totally wear one of those." Caroline's face writhed in pain as the tears fell harder. "I'm just kidding, Care. You can't worry about what other people would think. You're the one who has to live with your decisions, not them."

Caroline sniffed and put her head in her hands. "Before Jackson, I'd never thought about any guy other than Clay. I knew exactly what I wanted and where my life was headed."

Bailey's brown curls shook in understanding as Caroline continued. "But now that I've met Jackson, I am questioning everything. It's like nothing in my life will ever be the same, no matter what I do."

"I know. Look Care, this is a lot to deal with in two nights." Bailey stroked Caroline's long blonde hair and wished she could take her pain away.

"I am exhausted," Caroline admitted.

"I'm sure you are." Bailey smiled tenderly at her lifelong friend "And one last thing."

Caroline cocked her head to one side and muttered, "Yeah?"

"Sometimes other hearts have to break in order to keep yours intact."

Bailey's words shot straight to the source of Caroline's angst like a sharpened arrow. She felt them blow straight past her mind, down her throat, and bury themselves in the center of her chest. "That was deep, Bails." She took a deep breath. "Thank you."

"I love you, Care. This will all be okay. It will all work out."

"I love you, too. Thanks for being here with me." The girls hugged and Caroline's tears finally slowed.

"That's what best friends are for." Bailey gave her another squeeze. "But now it's my job—as your best friend, of course—to put your ass to bed."

Caroline snickered a little and walked slowly into Bailey's oversized bedroom. She was grateful for the escape. She was in no shape to be at home with Clay. Bailey had taken care of it all. She sent Caroline to the shower and then called Clay.

"You know how we girls get when it comes to weddings. Lots to plan and talk about!" Bailey could pull off any lie she needed to if it protected her friend, which worked out really, because Caroline was a terrible liar.

"I'll tell her. 'Night, Clay." Bailey hung up and wondered how the hell Caroline was going to make it out of this situation in one piece.

Caroline walked out of the bedroom and tried to dry her long wet hair with a towel when Bailey spoke up. "I called Clay. He knows you're here and staying the night. He said to tell you goodnight and he loves you."

Her eyes started to water again as Caroline struggled to keep her emotions in check. "Thank you so much, Bailey. There was no way I could have talked to him."

"I know."

Caroline grabbed her purse from off the couch, opened up the zipper compartment, and pulled out the note Jackson had sent her along with the heart charm. She ran her thumb across the words in the note, thinking of how his hand had also touched that paper.

Affection swirled within her as she placed the charm on the nightstand and crawled into the queen-sized bed. The paper firmly clutched to her chest, she quietly cried herself to sleep.

♡ Twelve

When Caroline woke up the next morning, emotions from the previous night flooded her mind like a hurricane. Everything felt exactly the same.

"Morning," Bailey said from her side of the bed.

"Hi."

"How do you feel?"

"Just as awful and confused as I did last night." Caroline's face crinkled. "But you know the worst part?" Her eyes filled up with tears.

"What?"

"All I keep thinking about is Jackson. Why hasn't he called, or texted, or something?"

Bailey smiled softly from her pillow. "I don't think that's the worst part."

Caroline stared at her friend. "God, I am so tired of crying. How is it possible I have any stupid tears left? This is ridiculous."

Bailey smirked. "You should try to call him. And you should do it now, while you're here and we can still buy you time with Clay."

Caroline nodded. "Okay."

Bailey stretched and let out a yawn. "I'll be in the other room if you need me."

"Thanks." Caroline reached across the bed toward the nightstand. She grabbed her phone and pressed the button to call Jackson. As it rang, her whole body began to shake uncontrollably. She was nervous. It rang more times than it had in the past six months. She thought he wasn't going to answer, but he did.

"Hello." His voice sounded ragged, tired, and beaten.

"Hi." She didn't even know where to begin. "How are you?" She wanted to kick herself after those words escaped her lips.

"Um, I'm pretty terrible, Caroline. How are you?" He was still angry, hurt, and bitter.

Her heart twisted into knots at the tone of his voice and made the bile in her stomach rise into her throat. "I'm a mess," she admitted.

"I don't want to play games." His voice sounded cold and uncaring.

That sentence instantly made her defenses rise. The hairs on the back of her neck stood up as anger spread throughout her body. "Then don't, Jackson." She spoke his name with disdain.

"Why are you calling, Caroline? What do you want?"

The harshness of his questions infuriated her. "Nothing. My mistake. Sorry to have bothered you. Have a nice life." She hung up and then hurled her phone at the bedroom wall. Thankful it didn't break, she slowly got up to retrieve it.

Suddenly her phone started to blare Jackson's ringtone and she considered briefly letting it go to voicemail just to make him suffer. But she couldn't do it. She answered with only a breath before Jackson immediately asked, "Don't you want to be with me?" His voice cracked with emotion.

She was quiet at first and knew he felt stupid when he quickly added, "Forget it. I shouldn't have asked. I shouldn't have called back."

"No! Jackson wait!" Caroline pleaded. "I do…want to be with you."

"You do?" His voice sounded lighter…hopeful.

"Of course I do," she stressed. "But it's not that easy."

"It *is* that easy, Caroline. You want something, then you do it. Why won't you just do it?"

"Do what? Leave Clay and be with you? Is that what you want?"

"Of course that's what I want. Isn't that what you want?" His voice sounded desperate.

"What would people say?"

"Who gives a shit what people would say? You're going to just stay in this relationship, marry this guy and have his kids, because you don't want to deal with what people might say if you leave him?" Jackson spat, his tone rising.

Silence thundered between them before Jackson spoke again. "You're not the person I thought you were."

"What is that supposed to mean?" She choked the words out through her obvious shock.

"I just never pegged you for the kind of girl who lived her life to please everyone else. It's pathetic, really." He spoke the last sentence with as much disdain as he could muster up.

"That's not fair." She wasn't going to sit there and let him talk to her like that. "It's easy for you to sit there and judge me when you're not the one who has to make the tough decisions."

"God damn it, listen to me," Jackson lashed out. "I want to be with you. I don't want you to marry this guy, no matter how great he is. And if you wanted to marry him, you wouldn't be having this conversation with me right now. Hell, we wouldn't have done anything that we've done the last six months."

"I know. It's just…"

He cut her off. "Let me finish."

She fell quiet as he continued. "I'm not sure I could live through you marrying someone else. I think about you all the time. And I think about *us* all the time. I want there to be an *us*, Caroline. We belong together. And if you'd stop worrying about what everyone else thought, you'd see that too."

Caroline leaned her head into the bed and tried to muffle the sound of her heart breaking. "I don't think I'm strong enough," she admitted softly.

"Strong enough…for what?" his voice faltered.

She paused a moment before answering, "To leave Clay."

The silence hung between them like thick smoke in a slow burning room, until Jackson choked out, "Caroline?"

"I'm here." She spoke the words so faintly, he barely registered the response.

"I'm in love with you."

It was the final blow. She broke down. "I just don't want to hurt anyone. And leaving Clay would hurt so many people."

"So I guess it's better you live your life unhappy so everyone else can be happy?"

"Don't be mean. It's not that," she fretted.

"Then WHAT is it? Tell me. Help me see what the hell it is that you're thinking? Make it okay for me that I let you go. God, Caroline, do you love me or not?" he asked half-crazed.

"Of course I love you. The thought of not being with you makes me feel like nothing will ever truly be right in my life again."

His heart beat wildly with hope against the confines of his chest. "When two people love each other, they should be together."

Filled with guilt, she asked. "At what cost? Any? That's so selfish. I can't live my life only thinking of myself with no regard for anyone else."

"No. You can't. But it's not like you're already married. You haven't taken that leap yet." His voice quivered as his tone changed. "I'm just asking you not to take it, Caroline. Because once you do that…well, I can't keep doing this. Not if you choose to marry him."

"Clay doesn't deserve this."

"But I do?"

"I never asked to meet you!" Caroline pulled the phone away from her face and yelled into the receiver. Once the words passed through her teeth she desperately wished she could stuff them back into her mouth and swallow them whole.

"As much as I'd love to say I didn't ask to meet you either, I can't." The dejection coursed from his lips to her ears. "I've waited my whole life to find someone like you."

"I didn't mean that Jackson, I'm sorry…"

"I know."

"It's just that I need to be able to look at myself in the mirror and like the person I see there. You understand that, don't you?"

"I do," he sighed.

"I just need a little time to figure this all out."

Caroline's stomach knotted with anticipation as she waited for his response.

"I can't wait." Jackson's words came out resolute mixed with disbelief.

"What do you mean, you can't wait?" Anger coursed through her body with the intensity of white-hot heat.

His feelings spilled out into the phone. "I can't just sit here and wait for you any more. I've been waiting for the last six months and look what it's got me…a girl with a ring on her finger and a completely shattered heart." His tone changed back to the cruel one meant to cause her pain.

"So what then? This is it? We end it just like this?" She spat back, her head pounding.

"I can't keep doing this to myself. It's torture. And it's not fair to me."

She felt the warmth of her anger dissipate as cold shock rapidly filled its place. "What about how I feel?"

"If you're not going to leave him, then it doesn't really matter how you feel, does it?" A breath tore from her mouth with a loud huff as her head shook with disbelief at his words.

"Goodbye, Caroline. I love you. Please don't call me any more." He hung up the phone before she could respond.

Caroline sat on Bailey's bed, staring at her cell phone. What the hell just happened and how did things go from him telling her he loved her, to saying goodbye forever?

"Bailey!!!" Caroline yelled out through her tears, which once again, fell uncontrollably down her cheeks.

The door swung open and Bailey ran into the room. "What happened?"

Caroline shook her head. "I don't know. One minute he was begging me not to marry Clay, telling me he loved me. And the next, he's telling me he can't keep doing this and not to call him ever again."

"He said that?" Bailey scrunched up her face and gave her a weird look.

"Yeah."

"Well, wait, hold on. Back up. He told you he loved you?" Bailey smiled.

"Among other things, yes."

"Did you tell him you loved him back?" Bailey grinned.

Caroline eyed her friend. "I did. Do you think I'm a bad person?"

"Of course not! But, oh my God! You love him?"

"I think I do." She shrugged her shoulders and then quickly recanted. "I mean, I know I do. I just don't know if it's real."

"What do you mean; you don't know if it's real? Of course it's real." Bailey reassured.

"Well, how do I know for sure? What if I'm just convincing myself that I love him? What if I'm imagining feelings that aren't based in reality?"

"I'm sorry, Caroline, but when in your life have you *ever* done that? And why *would* you? What would be the point?"

"I don't know, but he's not here and I don't have to see him every day—so what if that's why I think I like him so much?" Caroline shook her head and closed her eyes. "I feel completely out of control."

"Why?"

"Because it feels like my world is spinning a million miles an hour and I'm barely holding on."

"You can stop the spinning, you know. Or at least slow it down."

Caroline wished she believed Bailey, but she didn't.

"So how did it end? I mean, how did you guys get off the phone?" Bailey wondered.

"He basically hung up on me after saying not to call him again."

"Wow. He's got it bad." Bailey covered her heart with her hand and stuck out her bottom lip.

"What do you mean?" Caroline was tired of feeling clueless. "And why do I feel so stupid right now? I mean, shouldn't I be the one with all the answers? Why are you so insightful all of a sudden?"

"I've always been insightful, brat! You've just never needed my insight before because your life has always been perfect. Even when your choices were hard, you always knew exactly what you wanted, so no one could stop you. You never needed advice from anyone, because you never cared what anyone would tell you."

Bailey shook her head and went on. "I think that's the weirdest part for me with all of this. I just don't really get why this situation is so different for you."

"I think because I'm in so deep. Like I pushed for me and Clay to be here. I mean, there is no reason why Clay would feel like I wouldn't want to marry him, you know what I mean? This was always part of my plan."

Bailey interrupted her flow. "Until now..."

Caroline nodded her head in agreement and repeated, "Until now..."

"Well, listen. Jackson's just telling you that you guys can't talk any more because he's hurt. And having you in his life is too painful. Since you've agreed to marry your freaking boyfriend, he can't keep talking to you. That can only end badly for him. He's not winning this battle, so he has to bow out before it literally kills him."

"You should be a love counselor or something." She smiled at her beautiful friend.

"It's about time you appreciated my awesomeness," Bailey remarked.

"I do," Caroline said before she wrapped her arms around her friend's neck. "Thank you so much, Bailey."

♡ T h i r t e e n

Caroline mentally kept count of the number of days it had been since she and Jackson last talked. It surprised her that the pain in her heart never seemed to lessen as the days quickly turned into weeks.

The intercom blared and she looked down to see Bailey's extension number on the phone's monitor.

"What's up?"

Bailey's sympathetic tone asked, "Just making sure you're okay."

Caroline stared at the tan fabric lines of her cubicle wall. "I'm okay, thanks."

Bailey sensed her unease. "Still counting days?"

Caroline winced. "It's so hard, Bails. I guess I never realized how deeply he had become a part of me, you know? But it's like I can literally feel the emptiness inside of me now that he's gone." She paused and her voice turned into a whisper. "It hurts to breathe."

Bailey cringed. "I'm sorry, Care. I can't even imagine how much it hurts."

"I just really miss him."

"Caroline, this came for you." Caroline jerked and swung around in her chair as the receptionist placed a small white envelope on Caroline's desk.

"What was that?" Bailey asked.

"Lisa just dropped off a letter for me. Let me open it and I'll call you right back."

Her eyes lit up when she saw the "New York, NY" postage mark. She carefully opened the envelope and removed the paper from within. It read:

Dear Caroline,

I know now that I must truly let you go. As impossible as it seems, it feels even more impossible to do. The idea of living my life without you just feels wrong somehow, but I know it's what I have to do.

I've thought a lot about us these past few weeks. At first, I wanted answers as to why you came into my life if we weren't supposed to be together. It seemed so cruel, so unfair. Why would I get to meet and fall in love with you, if I didn't get to be with you?

I don't know…sometimes I think that we're like two ships passing in the night, aware of one another, but unable to come together. The current–too strong, the waves–too high, the weather–too stormy. If it was only one of those things, maybe we could have overcome it, but with all of them working against us at once, it was too difficult. Maybe if we had found each other in another time or place, things might have been different?

In all the pain however, there is hope. What you've given me, what you've made me feel. You brought me to life. I never knew I could feel so deeply for another. I never knew I could want to so badly. You've inspired me. And for that I am thankful.

I will always love you. I hope for your success and happiness. I wish so much that things were different for us, but I want you to know that I don't blame you. I'm not bitter. I understand the difficult position you are in and I'm so sorry for simplifying a situation that is clearly anything but simple.

Loving you and letting you go is probably the hardest thing I'll ever have to do. The fact that you are walking out of my life and down the aisle to another man is more painful than I can put into words. Just know that.

Forever Yours,

Jackson

Caroline struggled to catch the breath that lodged in her throat. His words sent deep fissures splintering through her already fractured heart. Desperately she attempted to read the letter again through blurred and watery eyes.

Her fingers trembled as she dialed Bailey's extension.

"Talk to me," Bailey answered.

"Get over here," Caroline whispered emotionally and promptly hung up.

Bailey handed the paper to Caroline. "Holy shit. This is…I don't even know what to say. How are you feeling? WHAT are you feeling?"

Tears spilled from Caroline's green eyes. "I don't know. Mostly sad, I think."

"How come?"

Caroline shrugged. "'Cause he's giving up. I mean, I know it's stupid to think he'd just be there forever. But he's letting go and that just…makes me sad." She tried in vain to wipe away the tears.

"It is sad," Bailey agreed.

"So, do I call him? Or text him? Or tell him I got the letter? What?"

"I wouldn't."

"Why not?"

"Because, Care. He just told you everything he wanted to say in that letter. You only want to call him because you've wanted to call him every day since that last phone call. You just think you have a reason now. But I think it would make things worse and you'd have to start all over again trying to feel better."

"This letter makes me have to start all over again!" Caroline's voice boomed with more intensity than she intended.

Bailey quickly scanned the office, looking at the raised heads of their co-workers and smiled. "Sorry," she covered for Caroline. Everyone turned back to their computer screens.

"Sorry," Caroline mumbled.

"It's okay. You know what, though?" Bailey paused as Caroline looked directly at her. "I think Jackson's right."

"About what?"

"Accepting the situation and letting it go. I mean, if you guys aren't going to be together," Bailey raised her eyebrows and dipped her head, "then there really is no other option. You can't keep holding on to something you said you didn't want."

Caroline grimaced.

"I'm not trying to be mean, Care. I'm just saying…"

"I know. You're right. It just hurts."

♡ Fourteen

Clay stopped the car on the stone-paved driveway and Caroline quickly hopped out of the passenger seat. She stretched her arms into the air and shouted, "I LOVE being home!"

Clay laughed. "The weather is so much warmer here."

"I miss it so much." Caroline glanced up at the blue sky dotted with puffy white clouds and smiled.

Clay grabbed Caroline's bags and closed the trunk. "I'll bring these to your room, okay?"

"Thanks, babe," she said as she followed him into the house. "Mom? Dad?"

"Maybe they're still shopping for the engagement party."

"You're probably right."

"Do you want me to wait with you until one of them gets back?"

"No, of course not. Go home. Tell your parents I said *hi* and I'll see you all tomorrow for the party."

"All right." Clay bent down and sweetly kissed her mouth. "I love you," he said as his eyes twinkled.

"I love you, too." She watched as Clay headed out the front door and felt relief wash over her.

****

Jackson stroked the dark mane as his horse's body moved with grace underneath his legs. He loved riding and it was the one thing he missed most on the days he lived in the city. With a gentle tug of the reins, Lily came to a slow stop and Jackson quickly hopped off. He nuzzled into the side of her brown face and gave her a quick pat. "Don't worry, Lil, I won't be long," he said gently as he tied her reins around a large tree.

Shattered boards and splintered pieces of wood littered the ground around him. He knelt in the dirt to get a better look. He scratched his head. "That's weird. It looks like it was broken right through."

A dark shadow crossed over him and he tilted his head toward the sky. Ominous charcoal-colored clouds lingered in the sky above him, looking angry and warring. They hardly moved in any direction and Jackson noticed how they increased in size as the color turned even darker. "Get to work before these clouds dump on you, idiot," he said out loud.

He quickly hammered at the broken boards and replaced the old shattered pieces with new, perfect ones. Subconsciously, his thoughts gravitated toward Caroline. The color of her green eyes drifted into his mind and he smacked the side of his head with his free hand. He winced at the self-inflicted blow. Pieces of conversations replayed until he shouted into the air around him, "Just leave me alone! You didn't want me! Get out of my head!" He slammed his boots into the dirt and pieces flew in every direction.

He hated that he had allowed himself to feel so much for someone who was never available to him. He also hated how he let himself believe that they could end up together. His heart had definitely convinced his mind that she would leave her boyfriend for him. And when she didn't—well, everything changed. He stopped believing in love. And even though he allowed himself to date Sally from the bar, he didn't allow himself to feel a single thing for her.

Rain started to fall lightly as Jackson finished up the final board. He fastened the tools back onto his belt and headed toward the horse that watched his every move. The rain fell harder as each drop crashed into a branch, or leaf, the sounds building to a crescendo all around him. Lily pulled tightly at the reins with a nervous whinny, her tugging only securing the knot further.

Jackson stroked her neck slowly, hoping to reassure her. "Okay, girl, we're leaving." He worked at the knot as lightning lit up the sky and thunder rumbled in the distance. Lily refused to keep her large body still, clearly spooked by the storm. Jackson continued to fight with the knot until it loosened. He quickly unwrapped the leather from the tree as lightning blasted through the sky and struck the ground in front of him.

He jumped back as Lily bucked violently and stood on her hind legs, half crazed. Jackson fought fiercely with her, but knew he was no match for a full-sized horse. She was out of control and Jackson did everything in his power to calm her and regain control. He wrapped the reins tightly around his hands.

"It's okay, Lily. Calm down. Calm down," he shouted through the battering storm. He held onto her reins as securely as he could. He tried to pull her head down and hold her steady, but she wouldn't stop bucking. Another bolt of lightning shot out from the now almost black sky and Jackson realized he couldn't hold on any longer.

He desperately tried to unwrap the reins he had just wrapped so tightly from around his hands. He knew that if he didn't get them undone quickly, Lily could take off and he would be powerless to do anything except drag along behind her.

Lily continued to buck and kick in fear as Jackson frantically tried to get loose. "Come on! Come on!" he screamed into the pounding rain and wind. "Almost got it," he thought as Lily kicked one final time with ferocity. He watched helplessly as her back leg came into view. "Lily, N-!" he screamed as his body suddenly slammed violently into the ground below. Blood spilled from the side of his head, mixing with the rain and dirt. Jackson lay there motionless as Lily ran off, dragging the loose reins behind her.

Jackson drifted in and out of consciousness. He tried to move, but didn't have the strength. The rain fell mercilessly against his face and stung whenever it struck the open wound in his head. He closed his eyes and wondered if anyone would come for him, or if he would die in that field, all alone.

Caroline's face flashed in his mind and this time he welcomed the image. She smiled as strands of sun-streaked blonde hair fell in front of her eyes. *I love you*, he heard her voice say. Instinctively, he reached out to touch her, but the image faded. As he drifted between states of awareness, all he could think about was *her*. His eyes slammed shut and blackness enveloped him.

****

Bailey bounced happily into Caroline's bedroom wearing a dark blue, knee-length dress. Caroline stopped fussing with her hair and turned. "Wow, Bails, you look stunning!"

Bailey twirled around. "Thanks! Now what's going on with you?"

"I don't know what the hell to do with my hair." Caroline turned back to the mirror.

"I'll do it for you," Bailey said as she reached for the hot curling iron.

"Thank God." Caroline watched as pieces of her long blond hair were twirled delicately around the heated iron.

"It's the last time I'll ask, I promise. But have you heard from him?"

"Not since that day."

"How long has it been?" Bailey tested.

"Almost twelve weeks."

"Still counting, eh? Well, that's healthy."

"Shut up." Caroline laughed.

"How are you holding up?" Bailey asked with an edge of seriousness.

"It's hard," Caroline admitted honestly, "Shouldn't I be freaking over him by now?"

"Maybe you'll never truly be over him…"

"Well, that sucks. Aren't you supposed to make me feel better? This IS my engagement party you know."

"Well, maybe you're engaged to the wrong guy."

Caroline whipped her head to glare at Bailey. "Ow!"

"Don't move! You can't whip your head around like that when I have your hair all tangled up."

"Bailey!" Caroline chastised.

"I'm kidding. Gosh, calm down," Bailey seemed nonchalant while she continued to fuss with Caroline's hair. "There. Perfect." She admired the reflection in the mirror.

"Oh, that does look nice." Caroline's usually slick straight hair had been transformed into varying lengths of thick, wavy curls. The sides were pulled back loosely with jeweled clips that sparkled. "Thank you."

Bailey helped her slip into her black party dress, making sure not to mess up her hair. Caroline dug around in her overly stuffed bag and pulled out a pair of silver heels still wrapped in plastic.

"Nice shoes," Bailey commented.

"I knew you'd like them."

They heard the doorbell ring and the sound of Clay's familiar voice, followed closely by the sound of his parents, echoed down the hall. "Show time," Caroline said and took Bailey by the arm.

Clay's jaw dropped when he saw Caroline walking toward him. "Wow, baby, you look gorgeous!"

She feigned a smile and leaned in to give him a quick peck on the cheek. "Thank you. You look quite handsome yourself," she said, admiring the charcoal gray dress pants that accompanied a surf brand button-down black shirt.

"Hi, Mr. and Mrs. Matthews. It's great to see you." She hugged both of his parents who beamed with approval.

"It's great to see you, Caroline. You look beautiful." The overly animated tone made the butterflies in Caroline's stomach come alive. Her knees started to weaken as nerves took over her previously calm body.

"Jan, is that you I hear?" Caroline's mom yelled from the kitchen.

"Yes it is, mother of the bride!" And with that, Clay's mom rushed through the kitchen door.

****

Lily galloped toward the farm and Jackson's father noticed immediately that his son was absent from the horse's back. He bolted out the front door and toward the horse that had finally slowed down to a nervous trot. "Lily...come here, Lil." He noticed the mud-covered reins dragging on the ground and his heart sank. He looked into the distance for his son, but there was no sign of him.

"Where's Jackson?" A slender woman shouted from the front porch toward her husband.

"I don't know. Something's not right, hon. Lily came back without him." His brown eyes narrowed with worry. "You stay here, I'll go find him."

He hopped onto the waiting horse and took off toward the far side of the property line where Jackson had been working. The rain dumped water at them with ferocious intensity as the lightning and thunder spooked Lily, even in a full gallop. "Jackson!" He screamed his son's name while he rode, hoping to hear anything in response.

"Where is he?" His father frantically turned his head in every direction, his eyes intensely scanning the surroundings. He rode to the broken fence, which he noted had been fixed, but still saw no sign of Jackson.

"Jackson!" He shouted and quickly quieted his breath as he strained to listen over the pouring rain and Lily's heaving breath. The horse led him near the tree where she had been tied and he noticed broken branches and upturned mud littered the ground. That's when he spotted him. Just a shoe, at first.

"Jackson?" His father leapt off the horse and ran over toward what he hoped was not his son's body. "Jackson! Oh my God, Jackson!" Jackson lay in a small pool of blood, still unconscious. Terrified at the sight and unsure of what to do, he reached for his cell phone and dialed 911.

"Hello? I need an ambulance at the Parks Ranch. My son is unconscious and he's bleeding from his head. What? I'll check." He bent down and grabbed his son's wrist.

"Yes, he has a pulse. I'm not sure how long he's been out. I don't know what happened; I found him like this. No, I won't move him. Hurry. Please." Tears started to fall from his eyes as for once in his life, he felt completely helpless. He disconnected the call and quickly called his wife.

"Honey. I found Jackson, but he's unconscious. Calm down. The ambulance is coming, but you're going to have to help them find us. We're at the far end of the property line. Where the broken fence was…do you remember where that is? Yes, near the old tree. Just wait for them. I don't know, honey. Calm down. I know. I love you too." He ended the call as soon as he could. He was too scared to deal with a frantic woman at the moment and he knew he would be useless at trying to calm her down.

****

Crowds of people milled throughout Caroline's parents' modest backyard where white tables were arranged, each one covered with a crisp white linen. A solitary white candle surrounded by blood red roses adorned the center of each, where matching red, silk napkins sat perfectly folded beneath hand-written table cards.

Caroline was stunned into silence, noting each new detail, her mouth constantly agape. "Our parents are insane," she whispered into Clay's ear.

"You don't like it?"

"It's so pretty. It's just a bit much, don't you think?"

Clay looked around. "I think it's perfect." He placed a careful kiss on the top of her head. "Your hair looks really pretty."

"Thanks, babe."

She held on to Clay's arm as they walked though the yard, thanking everyone for coming.

"I don't know half the people here," Caroline confided into Clay's ear.

"Me either."

"Is this what our wedding's gonna be like? A bunch of strangers sharing our special day?" Caroline's stomach started to roll.

He stopped walking and turned to face her. "No. We won't let it."

"Promise?"

"Promise." He kissed her hand. "I think I hear your phone," Clay said as he craned his neck in the direction of the house.

"That's weird. I thought I left it in my room." She strained to listen until she too heard it ringing. "I hear it, too. Oh well, they can leave a message."

"What if it's important?" Clay's mind always seemed to be on work. It didn't matter what they did, where they were, or what happened around them. He always made time for the office.

Caroline's mind instantly flashed to a scene in the future…*the two of them at a soccer game, watching their son play. Clay's phone rings and he once again apologizes for having to leave. He gives Caroline a quick kiss on the cheek before running off. All the while, their son is watching their dad leave his game for the umpteenth time.* Her heart breaks a little as the scene in her mind fades.

"You're right. I'll go see who it is." She knew it wouldn't be her office since they all knew she was out of town for the weekend. Nothing she did there was so important that it couldn't wait for her return.

She found her phone on a table near the back door, but didn't recognize the number that was displayed. Her heart dropped when she realized it was the same area code as Jackson's number. "Hello?" She quickly scooted inside the house for some privacy.

"Caroline?"

"Yes," she responded cautiously. "Who's this?"

"I'm sorry. This is Alex, I'm one of…"

She cut him off. "I know who you are. You're one of Jackson's friends. What's up, this isn't really a good time." She peered out of the glass door and glanced over at Clay, who shrugged his shoulders in her direction. She gave him a quick wave and a smile to ward off any worry and watched as Clay turned and continued his conversation.

"I'm sorry, but um…listen. Jackson got into a really bad accident. He's in the hospital and I just thought someone should tell you." Caroline's pulse quickened at the fear and worry in Jackson's friend's voice.

She walked into her room, closed the bedroom door, and sat on her bed. "What do you mean? What kind of accident? Is he okay?" The phone trembled in Caroline's hand and goose bumps rose on her bare arms.

"No, he's not okay; we don't know if he's going to make it. It was a pretty bad accident. He was at the farm on his horse. We're not sure what happened, but he's in a really bad way, Caroline. I just thought you should know."

Caroline's body numbed and her mind went blank. All she kept hearing in her head were Alex's words repeating, *"We don't know if he's going to make it."*

"Caroline? Are you there?" Alex stopped the words from playing in her mind one last time.

"I'm here. Where is he?" She swallowed her pride.

"Albany Memorial."

"Okay."

"He loves you, you know."

"I know," she admitted.

"Okay. Well, I just figured someone ought to tell you," Alex explained with an uncomfortable edge to his otherwise kind voice.

"Thank you so much, Alex. I really appreciate it."

She hung up, her mind instantly filled with clarity. The idea of staying at this stupid party she never wanted in the first place seemed beyond ridiculous. How could she celebrate anything when Jackson was possibly dying in a hospital room on the other side of the country?

Afraid the guilt might stop her, she refused to over-analyze what she was about to do. But the truth—her truth—could no longer be denied. She promptly changed out of her dress and into more comfortable clothes. She grabbed her purse and a jacket, and then went outside to look for Clay.

She spotted his confused expression as he rushed to meet her. "What's going on? Where are you going?" He took in her change of clothes with a disapproving glance.

"I'm so sorry, Clay, but I have to go."

His brows furrowed in confusion. "What do you mean, you have to go? Where are you going? Caroline? What's going on?"

"I'm sorry. I'll tell you everything later, I promise. I'll call you." She ran toward the front of the house, refusing to look back.

She heard her mother shout, "Caroline, honey, where are you going?"

Pangs of guilt coursed through her as the beautiful party decorations and the trouble her parents had gone to flashed in her mind. But she didn't stop running. She couldn't. She'd explain it all to her parents later and prayed they'd understand.

Bailey stood next to a buffet table and watched the scene unfold with a bright gleam in her eyes. She brought her wine glass to her lips and hesitating, lifted it in a subtle toast to Caroline, before taking a satisfied sip.

As Caroline drove to the airport, the realization that she had left Clay alone in her parents' back yard to pick up the pieces of her disappearance hit her. Thankfully, it was brief before it was hastily replaced by thoughts of Jackson. She parked her car, raced inside, and inquired about the next flight to New York.

Luck, fate, or whatever you want to call it seemed to be on her side as the ticket agent informed her that seats were still available on the next flight. "Perfect. I'll take one."

She pulled out her "for emergencies only" credit card and charged the one-way ticket on it. Her stomach flipped at the thought of a five-hour flight. She heard Alex's voice repeating how Jackson *wasn't okay*. They weren't sure what happened, but he was *in a bad way*.

How could she have been so stupid? How could she have tried to pretend these past few months that none of it mattered…that there was no Jackson Parks? She would never forgive herself if something happened to him.

The *ping* of an incoming text broke her concentration. "*What's up?*"

Bailey's question forced Caroline to remember the party she had just ditched…and Clay. She'd never go through with this flight if she allowed herself to think about the upcoming consequences of her actions.

She responded, "*So sorry, Bails, Jax is in the hospital and apparently he's not okay. Flying to Albany now.*" Five seconds after she hit *Send* her phone rang, making her jump from the ringtone that played.

"What? What happened to him?" Bailey freaked.

"I don't know. I got a call from one of his friends telling me that he was in the hospital and that he was in a bad way. A BAD WAY, Bails. How could I have been so stupid?"

"You're not stupid. And just for the record…you're doing the right thing."

Bailey's reassurance gave Caroline a brief moment of peace. "Thank you. Oh geez, how's Clay?"

"Confused, of course. But he'll be fine. Leave him to me. I'll tell him I talked to you and you got some crazy phone call about someone being hurt in New York and you had to go ASAP."

"He'll think it's Tray."

"I know."

"But then he'll want to fly out." The last thing Caroline wanted or needed was Clay flying out half-crazed to New York under false pretenses.

"I know. But he can't. He's on a big case, remember," Bailey said through her sarcasm.

Caroline sighed. "Bailey, I have to go. We're boarding already."

"Hang in there. It will all be okay. I'm proud of you."

"Thanks. I needed to hear that."

She sat down in her assigned seat and realized it was the first time she'd been on a plane since she and Jackson had met. The emotions from that day immediately flooded through her and she thought she might pass out.

She sunk deeper into her seat and tried to fight off the bad feelings she couldn't seem to shake. What if he died? She reached into her purse and gently pulled out the heart charm from Jackson, which she secretly had affixed to a long silver chain. She unclasped the necklace for the first time and fastened it securely around her neck. She felt the chill of the metal against her skin as it rested underneath her shirt.

She wrapped her arms tightly around herself and forced her eyes to close.

♡ Fifteen

When Caroline awoke, she spent the remainder of the flight beating herself up emotionally. Life was too short and too precious to waste making decisions you didn't really want. Of course other people's feelings should be taken into consideration, but their wants and needs shouldn't be more important than your own. And then she heard Bailey's words in her head, *"Sometimes other hearts have to break in order to keep yours intact."*

She nodded to herself and the truth resonated within every fiber of her being. She also recognized that it was far easier said than done, but there was no time for that. After landing, she hailed a cab for the fifteen-minute drive to the hospital.

Caroline practically sprinted into the large white building before she spotted a guy walking down the hall that instinct told her was Alex. She shouted his name and the guy stopped walking and turned around.

"Are you Alex?"

"Caroline?" Alex immediately recognized her voice.

"Yeah," she responded, half out of breath.

He walked over to her with a smile on his face. "I can't believe you're here. Thanks for coming."

"Where is he?" she asked, every drop of her strained emotions spilling out in her words. "Is he alive?"

"He's alive." Alex put a hand on her shoulder. "He's over here."

Caroline's eyes softened. "I love him too, you know."

"I do have to warn you, though. I, um, didn't know you were coming. And, well…"

"What is it?" Nervous energy shot through her and stopped her legs from taking another step.

"It's just that…Sally's here. That's the girl he's been dating the last couple of months or so."

"Oh." Caroline brought her fingers to her mouth and started to bite nervously on her nails. "I see." It had never even occurred to her that Jackson would have moved on so quickly.

"No. It's not…" Alex touched her shoulder and gave a gentle nudge forward. "He doesn't love her. But she wants him to. Anyway, she really cares about him, so it will probably rattle her a little to have you here."

"Got it." She exhaled and held her head up high.

"I knew you loved him back." He gave her a one-armed hug and winked at her playfully.

Alex held the door open for Caroline and she walked through, unsure of what to expect on the other side. She gasped at the sight of Jackson's body lying helplessly in the small hospital bed. Tubes and wires came from what seemed like every part of his exposed body. Machines beeped with a steady pace. His head was swollen to a size she couldn't describe and his arms and legs were bandaged in various places.

Her heart seized at first, but then love rapidly soared through her every fiber. She knew in that moment that everything she had felt for him all those months ago was real. It had always been real.

"I can't believe *you're* here." Tommy jerked his head in her direction and glared with disgust.

"You must be Tommy. I've heard you're not my biggest fan." Caroline attempted to be civil.

"Well, at least you came. I guess that says *something* about your character." His eyes rolled as he looked away.

"I guess I deserve that," she said as she tried to hide the sting of his words from her expression. Caroline looked over at the petite brunette sitting in the corner. "You must be Sally?" she said kindly, and offered a soft smile.

"I'm out of here," Tommy snorted as he stormed out of the room.

Alex shot Caroline an apologetic look. "I'll go talk to him."

Once the door shut, Sally stated, "And you must be the reason why he won't love me." She looked Caroline over from head to toe before continuing. "You know…I thought in time, he'd get over you." She took a breath for strength. "But he never did."

Caroline's gaze fell to the floor. "I'm sorry."

"You ruined him. All I wanted was for him to stop thinking about you and open his eyes to see me. ME!" Sally pounded at her chest with clenched fists. "I've been standing in front of him all along. I'd do anything for him. But he never cared. He never saw anyone but you. And I hate you for that." She dropped her face into her hands and wept.

Caroline struggled to catch the breath that escaped her. Her bottom lip quivered as she tried in vain to wipe away her tears. "I don't know what to say other than I'm so sorry. I never meant for any of this to happen."

"You broke his heart." Sally rose from the padded chair and gathered her belongings, her blue jeans and pink T-shirt wrinkled from sitting in one place for too long.

"Please don't go," Caroline pleaded.

Sally stopped and looked at her. "I don't belong here any more. I never did."

Caroline's eyes widened, her mouth agape. "Yes, you do. If anyone doesn't belong here, it's me."

"But he loves *you,* not me. Trust me, I've been reminded of that fact on more than one occasion," Sally insisted, deep sorrow evident in her eyes.

"But *you* love him. Please stay," Caroline insisted.

Sally sat back down in the chair and looked at Caroline with surprise.

"Thank you." Caroline's face relaxed. "I'm sure it hasn't been easy for you the past couple of months. I've been a complete idiot, but you…you've done nothing wrong…"

"…except fall in love with the wrong guy." Sally's voice quivered as she fought back tears.

Caroline walked over to the fragile girl and gently squeezed her hand. "Or the right one. I am really sorry for everything. I hope one day you can forgive me."

Sally took a long, deep breath before she looked into Caroline's tired eyes. "It means a lot to me that you care."

"It means a lot to me that you don't want to kill me," Caroline joked and raised her eyebrows.

"Oh, don't worry. I do," Sally remarked with a quick laugh.

"Just make sure it's quick and painless, please. Not a big fan of pain," Caroline shot back through clenched teeth.

"I'll keep that in mind." Sally's eyes locked with Caroline's for an uncomfortable beat, then she shrugged and smiled.

Waves of relief washed over Caroline as the tension began to alleviate. "I'm exhausted and I could really use a coffee. Can I get you one?"

"That would be nice. Thank you."

Caroline smiled and headed out the door. She surprised herself by finding the cafeteria without getting lost. She took a tentative sip of her coffee and closed her eyes tightly, enjoying the bold flavor that rushed through her.

She balanced the two scalding hot cups with her hands as her hip bumped against the door. It finally budged and she scooted quickly through the opening. "I wasn't sure how you took it, so I brought some cream and sugar." She handed Sally one of the steaming cups.

"Thanks again," Sally said as she grabbed two of the sugar packets. "I get it now."

"Get what?" Caroline cocked her head to the left and narrowed her eyes.

"Why he couldn't get over you. The way you looked at him when you walked into the room tonight. I've known Jackson my whole life, and I've never heard him talk about any girl the way he talks about you."

Her heart soared within her chest, but she didn't let it show. "It took me getting that phone call to realize where I was supposed to be," Caroline freely admitted.

"He said you have a fiancé, right?" Sally glanced down at Caroline's ring finger, which still bore the enormous diamond ring Clay had given her.

"Yeah. But I did just walk out of my own engagement party to come here." Caroline shrugged.

"No, you didn't? Did you really?" Sally's mouth was agape.

"I did."

"Guess leaving him at the engagement party is better than leaving him at the altar, right?"

The smile dropped from Caroline's face almost immediately as the weight of Sally's words crashed around her.

"Oh gosh, Caroline, I'm sorry. I didn't mean anything by it." Sally put her hand over her heart and furrowed her brow.

"No. I know. It's just..." An awful awareness surged through Caroline. "What kind of person walks out of their own engagement party?"

"The kind that isn't happy to be there?" Sally remarked.

Caroline's hand covered her mouth as her eyes closed. "I'm a terrible person," she said under her breath.

Sally hesitated before adding, "No, you're not, but can I ask you something?"

"Of course." Caroline nodded.

"Do you love him?" Sally's gaze turned toward Jackson's still form.

Without hesitation, Caroline proclaimed, "I do."

"He's a really great guy. I'd tell you not to break his heart, but you've already done that, so…" The girls' laughter echoed through the room as Tommy and Alex walked back in.

"How long are you staying, anyway?" Tommy asked in Caroline's direction, his tone still clearly annoyed.

"I don't know? I hadn't even thought about it really. A few days, I guess?" She realized she hadn't thought this trip through very well.

Tommy groaned and Alex hit him in the arm. "Caroline, don't listen to him. It's good that you're here." Alex smiled.

"Where are his parents?" Caroline asked.

"Mr. Parks took the missus back home to get some rest and grab some of their things. They're going to stay in the hotel across the street for a while. They should be back later." Alex stared at Jackson.

"How long can we stay?" Caroline noted the time.

"We don't really know." Alex answered as he looked around.

"So what is his condition exactly? Do we know?" Caroline inquired.

"What's his condition? He's preparing for the Olympics, genius." Tommy could barely contain his apparent dislike for Caroline.

"Dude!" Alex's face flushed a rosy color as he shook his head in exasperation.

Sally stood up calmly and announced, "I could use a walk. Come with me?" She motioned toward Tommy.

He rolled his eyes in defiance. "I just got back in here!"

Sally linked her arm in his. "Just come with me anyway. Please?" Tommy's hard facade softened as he took in Sally's earnest expression. He lowered his head and reluctantly walked out of the room.

Alex's face was still red. "I am so sorry for Tommy. He um…"

"…hates me?" Caroline offered.

Alex laughed and insisted, "No!" Then he conceded, "Well, yeah. He hates you."

Disappointment filtered through Caroline's awareness. "It's okay. I totally get it."

Caroline walked up to the charts that surrounded Jackson. There were notes scribbled and numbers written that made no sense to her. "So, what does all this mean?"

Alex tried to recite in less confusing terms what the doctors had explained to him earlier. "He's in a medically induced coma for now. They say it's the best way to help him recover, but it's tricky and he needs to be constantly monitored."

Caroline nodded that she understood and he continued. "Basically, they shut his brain down. Once the swelling starts to go down, they'll lower the medications that are keeping him in the coma. But until that happens, he has to stay like this."

"So why does he have all these other wires and things on him? It looks like he isn't doing anything on his own." Caroline's voice trembled.

Alex's voice softened, soothing Caroline's fears. "Don't worry. When they put him in the coma, they had to give him things to keep his blood pressure down. And make sure his heart still pumped properly. They shut down his brain, remember? So all the things it did for his body, they have to do."

Caroline understood, but it still sounded scary and overwhelming. "Got it. So how long will it take the swelling to go down?"

Alex shook his head. "They can't say. It could be days…or weeks. No one knows."

A nurse walked through the door and looked at the clock on the wall as she began to take Jackson's vitals. "I'm sorry, you guys, but visiting hours are over. You're welcome to come back tomorrow morning at seven."

Caroline turned to grab her things. "Where are you staying?" Alex asked.

"I have no idea," she said, before a yawn crept out.

"You can stay in Jackson's room," he offered.

"What about Sally?"

"She won't even leave the hospital."

Caroline's eyes widened. "Seriously?"

Alex's expression mimicked hers. "Seriously."

"Tommy's gonna flip out," she remarked with a straight face.

Alex laughed. "Probably."

"I really appreciate it. Thank you." It seemed wrong somehow to go to Jackson's home without him, but she looked forward to being surrounded by his things.

After some convincing, which came mostly in the form of Tommy and Alex yelling at each another, Tommy agreed that Caroline could stay at their place for the night. She overheard him shout, "Just keep her away from me!" His tone made her shudder.

Once inside their apartment, Tommy walked to his room and slammed the door shut. Caroline looked visibly uncomfortable as Alex apologized. "I don't even know what to say about him any more. Here, this is Jackson's room." He opened the door for her. "And he has an attached bathroom so you don't have to use the one in the hall."

The tension in her face subsided. She threw her arms around Alex's neck and hugged him tightly. "Thank you so much, Alex. For everything."

Alex's cheeks turned bright red. "This is what Jackson would want. Make yourself at home. Goodnight, Caroline."

"Goodnight."

Alex stopped in the hallway and shouted, "Oh yeah. Hey, we leave here between seven and seven thirty."

"Thanks," she yelled through the closed door.

Once in the silence of Jackson's bedroom, she looked around, taking note of everything that surrounded her. There was simplicity that Caroline felt suited him perfectly. The color scheme was earthy, in natural tones of deep, dark browns and tans. His room was clean and uncluttered, aside from the two shirts that lay crumpled on the floor.

A small bookcase filled with books on history, farming, and even some classic literature sat against the wall. The dresser was tall and housed a large flat screen television on top. A simple nightstand with one drawer resided next to his queen-sized bed. A lone burgundy-colored candle sat on top of it, along with his alarm clock and iPod player.

She noted the candle's wick was still perfectly white. "Never been lit," she mumbled to no one as her hand ran across the still even top.

She sat down on the edge of his bed as the scent of him instantly surrounded her. She grabbed at the pillows, pulled them to her face and breathed him in. There would be no escaping him tonight.

Her mind wandered to impure thoughts of Sally and Jackson when a knock on the door broke her concentration. "Come in." She sighed, uncertain who would be there.

Alex poked his head around the door. "Sorry, Caroline, I just wanted to let you know that the sheets are clean."

Caroline let out a huge sigh of relief. "I was actually *just* thinking about that," she admitted.

"Sally hasn't been here for a while. Jackson went to her place mostly." Alex stopped short of revealing any more.

Caroline understood. "Thank you, Alex."

"Good night." He shut the door behind him.

Caroline washed her face and brushed her teeth before crawling into Jackson's bed and allowing the smell of him to engulf her. Once in his bed her eyes fell upon his nightstand. She thought briefly about lighting the candle, but knew it wasn't her place.

She noticed something barely peeking out from the drawer. She knew better than to snoop, but curiosity got the best of her. She pulled it open without a sound and the picture of her and Jackson from the plane fell back inside. She ran a finger across the image of his face, as her passion surged.

The flashing light on Caroline's cell phone drew her attention away from the picture. Her heart instantly felt like it weighed a thousand pounds inside her chest. She scrolled through her text messages and missed phone calls, her burden deepening with each one. Slowly, she pressed the digits to her mom's cell phone. Her mom answered immediately, her voice filled with concern.

"I know, Mom. I'm so sorry for leaving like that. Yes, I'm in New York. Of course I'll be back soon. I know. I'll apologize to Clay's parents, as well."

She took a deep breath. "I can't explain it all right now, Mom, but I promise to fill you in. I know, I'm sorry. No, I'm not in any trouble. No, I haven't talked to Clay yet. I know…,I'll call him."

She took another deep breath. "Yes, I'm okay. I'm really sorry, Mom. I know. I'll call you soon. I love you too. 'Bye."

Unable to fathom having another conversation, she set her phone to "alarm only" and fell asleep wrapped in Jackson's essence.

****

Caroline, Sally, Alex, and Tommy sat in various chairs around the hospital room when Jackson's parents walked through the door. Jackson's mom instantly started crying at the sight of her only son and his father reached his arms around his wife to comfort her. His mother looked up in Caroline's direction and gathered her composure. "Oh, hello there. I don't think we've met?"

Caroline stood up with a smile and reached out her hand. She noticed the same heart charm that Jackson had sent to her, fashioned on top of a ring his mother wore. "I'm Caroline. I'm a friend of Jackson's," Caroline said politely.

Tommy cleared his throat and Caroline shot him a nasty glare. "Do you know Jackson from school? Or the city or something?" his mother inquired.

Caroline felt her face flush with embarrassment. "No, ma'am. We met on a flight almost a year ago." Caroline felt like a complete idiot at the admission.

Mrs. Parks' expression reflected shock and confusion. "Oh. Well, thank you for coming."

She walked over to Sally with a huge grin on her face. "Oh, Sally. Thank you so much for being here. I know it will mean the world to Jackson when he wakes up." The two hugged like old friends.

Tommy could barely contain his laughter as he attempted to hide the devilish grin on his face with his hands. And

Alex's face, in his discomfort, had turned bright red. Neither had realized that Jackson's parents didn't know who Caroline was.

Caroline desperately wanted out of that room. "If you'll excuse me, I really need to use the restroom." She jerked open the door, practically busting it off its hinges on her way out.

Caroline ran around the corner and threw the bathroom door open with an exasperated breath. She flung open a stall door and quickly locked it behind her. She sat on top of the seat, buried her face in her hands and gasped for air. Tears spilled over her fingers as she berated herself. What was she doing there? His parents didn't even know who she was! She didn't belong there. She wasn't his best friend, or the girl he was dating, or anything to him. How could she have been so stupid?

"Oh my God," she said out loud as the most awful of realizations slammed down on top of her.

What if Jackson didn't want her there?

Caroline realized at that moment she had to go back to San Francisco. Her ego had allowed her to simply assume that Jackson could never get over her the same way she couldn't get over him. She had convinced herself that he still wanted her, when she didn't know that to be the truth at all.

She wiped her eyes with the backs of her hands and pulled herself together. She exhaled and walked out of the bathroom toward the nurse's station. "Excuse me?" Caroline spoke to the middle-aged woman behind the counter.

"Yes?" the nurse asked, her eyes weary. "Can I help you?"

"Do you have a pad of paper and a pen I can borrow? I'll give it right back as soon as I'm done."

The nurse smiled. "Of course. Here you go." She handed her a legal-sized notepad and a pen with yellow smiley faces.

Caroline walked over to the empty seats along the wall across from the nurses' station and sat down to write Jackson a letter, just like he had once done for her all those months ago. Tears fell onto the paper, but she never stopped. Her heart spilled into her words. Everything came out on that page.

When she was done writing, she handed the notepad back to the nurse and asked if she could trouble her for an envelope. The nurse handed her one and Caroline carefully wrote "Jackson" on it with a small heart at the end. "Thank you so much," she said to the nurse before she returned the pen and walked toward Jackson's room.

Alex waited outside the door for her return. "I'm sorry about that, Caroline. You okay?"

Caroline forced a smile. "I will be. Random question for you…"

"Shoot," Alex said.

"The ring his mom is wearing—the one with the heart—where's it from?"

"Oh, the separated heart?"

Caroline nodded.

"It's cool, right? It's been in his family for generations. I think it was his great, great, great grandfather who made the first one. I think the story goes, if I'm remembering it right, that his grandfather kept trying to make his girlfriend a heart design, but he couldn't get the two halves to match up perfectly. No matter what he did, the right half was always longer than the left half. And he was never happy with the top of the heart where the halves came together. He couldn't weld the pieces just right and it always got like this big clump at the top.

"So one day, he took the latest heart he had made, where the top didn't quite come together and the right side hung lower than the left, and gave it to her anyway. He told her that it was better than a regular heart because it was separated and separated hearts were stronger than hearts that weren't. Apparently she thought it was the most beautiful thing she'd ever seen and asked if he could make a ring with it. And the design has been in their family ever since."

Caroline's face softened, picturing the scene in her mind. "That's a great story."

Alex smiled. "I think so, too. Why do you ask?"

"I was just wondering," Caroline evaded.

"Wait, did Jackson make one for you?" Alex asked with wide eyes. Caroline looked at him without answering. "He did, didn't he?" Alex asked again as Caroline reached for the chain buried under her shirt.

"He sent me the heart for my birthday. But I added the chain," she admitted.

"Wow," Alex responded. "That's a big deal."

"It is?" she questioned.

"Yeah," he told her. "It's tradition that each one of the Parks men put the heart on something, but they don't ever give it to just any girl. It's usually the girl they want to marry. And it doesn't have to be a ring, but I think that's what they all normally do. I know that all the women in his family have similar rings."

Caroline caressed the charm. She basked in the warmth she felt inside with the charm's newfound meaning.

"Jackson had to make that for you, you know? That's part of the tradition, too. If any Parks man wants to give the design to someone, they have to forge it themselves."

"That just makes it even more special," Caroline said, glowing. Knowing that Jackson had made it with his own two hands definitely changed the way she saw it. Not to mention, the way she felt about it.

Alex looked down and noticed the note in her hand. "You're going to leave, aren't you," he asked, more a statement than a question, breaking Caroline's train of thought.

"Let's just go back inside," she suggested.

"I'm going to grab some water. I'll be right back. Want anything?" Alex asked before he headed down the hall.

"No, thank you."

Caroline walked through the doors and only Sally remained inside. She held onto Jackson's hand and caressed it, but stopped when she saw Caroline.

"I think I'm going to go back home."

"When?" A slight smile escaped from Sally's lips as her eyes lifted.

"Today."

"So soon?"

"I need to get back to work. And I really need to talk to my fiancé and tell him everything that's going on. I've been avoiding him since I got here and that's not fair to him." Thinking about Clay made Caroline feel doubly worse.

"I have no right to ask you this, but when he wakes up, can you make sure he gets this?" Caroline held out the envelope.

Sally smiled and took it in her hand. "Of course."

"Thank you, Sally. I understand why he likes you, too."

The girls hugged briefly. Caroline walked to Jackson's bedside and was suddenly afraid to touch him. He looked so damaged. She gently lifted one of his hands and kissed the top of it. Then she bent toward his ear and whispered, "I love you. Please get better," softly enough that no one else could hear.

With one last look in Sally's direction, Caroline waved and quickly headed into the hallway. She almost ran smack into Alex, who was holding a tray filled with donuts and bagels.

"Where are you going?" His voice dropped.

"I've got to head back. I shouldn't be here," she confessed.

"Don't let his mom upset you. He doesn't tell her everything about his life, especially when he's brokenhearted." Alex tried to help her understand.

Caroline smiled, grateful for Alex and the kind of friend he was to Jackson. "I need to go home. Explain everything to Clay and stuff. If he opens his eyes, will you please let me know?"

He hugged her awkwardly, trying not to tip over the tray. "Of course."

Tommy rounded the corner and let out an annoyed grunt. "Isn't this cute?"

"I was just leaving, so you can go back to being your usual happy self," Caroline snapped back and walked out of the lobby.

♡ Sixteen

Caroline's rattled nerves kept her from sleeping the entire five-hour flight back to San Francisco. She tried to figure out exactly what she was going to tell Clay, but everything sounded wrong. She felt like a horrible, rotten person. Her emotions were in overdrive. Her body shook as the gravity of her guilt consumed her.

Her legs felt like anchors as she walked up the stairs to their apartment and slowly opened the door. She had half hoped he wouldn't be home, but Clay sat alone at their kitchen table. He looked like he'd been crying. His hair was a complete mess and she felt sick for having caused him pain.

"Are you going to tell me what's been going on? Is Tray okay?" His voice sounded exasperated and there was a longing she didn't recognize.

He still thought Caroline had been in New York to see Tracey? Caroline cursed Bailey silently for not telling him that part. "Tray's fine. I'm so sorry for leaving our party like that."

"Yeah, what was that? Why did you have to leave like that? What happened?" The details didn't add up for Clay and Caroline knew it.

She mustered up all of her strength and courage. "We need to talk."

Clay's eyes fell flat. "That's never a good sign."

Caroline started with, "Clay. You know I love you, right?"

Clay's jaw tightened and his eyes misted. "Of course I do," he said and reached out to stroke her arm.

"I can't do this." And with those words, Caroline lost it. The tears started to fall rapidly and she could barely stand the pain she was about to cause.

"Can't...do what?" Clay's voice hitched.

"I can't marry you," she whispered. She couldn't bring herself to say the dreaded words any louder.

"What do you mean you can't marry me?" He stood up from the chair and paced nervously back and forth.

She watched him before she answered. "I mean, I can't. I don't want to." She never intended to say it so harshly. She wanted to lessen the blow as much as possible, but telling a guy you don't *want* to marry them? There's no easy way to do that.

"You don't *want* to? Since when? You're just getting cold feet, right?" His questions flew out in desperation.

"I don't think so."

"You don't think so, but you aren't sure. So maybe it is just cold feet. Why don't you sleep on it and we'll see how you feel in the morning?" he demanded.

"I've been sleeping on it for the past three months!" she blurted out.

The energy in the room immediately shifted. Clay stopped pacing. "Oh," was all he could say. The devastation was written all over his face as his eyes started to glisten. He fell to his knees and Caroline could barely stand to watch.

"I'm so sorry, Clay, I never meant to hurt you. I just…things changed, I guess. *I've* changed."

He looked up from the floor. "How have you changed? How did this happen? I don't understand." His voice trailed off as he continued. "We were fine in New York…and we were fine here. But then Johnny died and you've never really been the same. But it can't be that. And then there was that guy from baggage claim." He paused as understanding dawned.

"Is there someone else?"

She couldn't bear the thought of inflicting more pain on someone as undeserving of it as Clay. Eventually she would tell him the whole truth, but it couldn't be tonight. Not right now. "Of course not," she lied through her teeth as bile churned in the pit of her stomach.

"Then, what happened? How can we fix this?" His desperate pleas filled the space between them.

Tears fell, her head shook, and she forced the words out. "We can't. I'm so sorry."

"No!" Clay's face reddened and his eyes narrowed in disgust. "You don't just wake up one day and not want to marry me. Something happened. Something had to have happened!"

Prickles of fear crept across her skin. She'd never heard Clay's voice so angry before. "Nothing happened, Clay. I don't know."

"This is bullshit! You're lying. I know you're lying!" His anger quickly grew.

"I'm not! Getting married doesn't feel right any more and you deserve so much better than that. Clay, you deserve someone who loves you and wants to marry you and be with you forever."

"That used to be you." As quickly as it entered his body, the anger subsided. Hurt took its place as tears rolled down his cheeks, the crimson color fading with each breath.

"I know," she sniffed. "I'm so sorry." She pulled the ring from her finger and placed it in the palm of his hand.

He clenched his fingers into a fist tightly around it. "I don't want this. I just want you."

Caroline fought off the sick feeling that rose in her stomach.

"Why are you doing this?" Clay begged.

"I'm so sorry, Clay. I'll stay at Bailey's tonight and then I'll pack my things during the week while you're at work."

"I can't believe this is happening. I never imagined…"
His voice turned soft and he mumbled things Caroline
couldn't quite make out.

She couldn't get out of there fast enough. Once in the
darkened narrow hallway, her emotions took over. What had
she done? For a brief moment, she actually contemplated
running back into the apartment and telling Clay she didn't
mean any of it. She would beg for his forgiveness and
everything would return to normal. Her mind screamed at her
to remove the chaos and pain. It wanted her to go back to
where things were comfortable and easy.

She tried to steady her racing heartbeat by breathing in
slow, deep breaths. With her hands on her knees, she
acknowledged that amidst all of this turmoil, a small part
within her dazzled with joy. Her life was no longer a road on
a map she could clearly see. She was on a new path, full of
endless opportunities and possibilities.

The black iron railing offered support for her trembling
hands. Everything she had once planned for and thought she
wanted with Clay, disappeared in the distance. And as she
watched it all fade away in her mind, she realized that fear
was absent. In its place resided hints of excitement. And she
knew in that moment that she had done the right thing.

Still trembling, she walked down the three flights of
marble stairs to her car. Once safely inside, she called Bailey.
"That didn't take very long," Bailey noted.

"I know. I thought he would fight with me a lot more, but
I think maybe he's in shock? I don't know. It was awful. And

even though I'm the one who did this, I feel sick to my stomach."

"Love isn't all rainbows and unicorns all the time. And neither is life. Sometimes life is really freaking hard."

"I still feel like shit. Just remind me that I'm not a terrible person, okay?" Caroline trembled.

Bailey's voice rose in volume and strength. "You're NOT a terrible person, Caroline Weber. Do you hear me? What would be terrible would be if you married someone you didn't love with all your heart. That's not fair to either of you. And it's selfish."

Caroline sniffed and her eyes burned. "Thanks, Bails. Be there in five."

"I'll wait outside for you."

Bailey hugged Caroline the moment she exited her car. "I know it's hard. You're doing the right thing."

Caroline tried to nod. "I feel so bad, though. You have no idea."

"That's because you're leaving your comfort zone. You're leaving the predictable and heading into the unknown. That's always scary."

"It's not that though, Bails. I don't feel bad for me. I - mean, I seriously want to kick my own ass for hurting Clay like this."

"You could always change your mind." Bailey let out an exasperated breath.

Caroline winced. "I don't want to change my mind."

Bailey smiled. "See. It's the right thing then. How's Jackson?"

Caroline sat on Bailey's oversized sofa chair and curled into a ball. "He's in a medically-induced coma. His head is so swollen, it's terrifying. The doctors have to wait for the swelling to go down before they can even try to wake him up."

"That sounds scary."

"It was. Seeing him like that—" Caroline shuddered— "was really hard."

"Did you meet his parents and stuff?"

"They didn't even know who I was," Caroline said as her eyes dropped.

"Shit. You're kidding? I'm sorry, Care."

Caroline shrugged her shoulders and grabbed a nearby pillow before holding it against her stomach. "I just didn't expect that, you know?"

Bailey's eyes lit up as she put the pieces together. "Is that why you came back so soon?"

Caroline avoided her friend's curious eyes. "Partly."

"Mostly."

Caroline looked up. "Mostly."

Bailey gave her a squeeze. "I love you. You will be okay. All of this will work out. I know it's hard right now, but it won't be forever."

"I sure hope you're right." Caroline closed her puffy eyes, hoping for any sliver of solace.

♡ **Seventeen**

Caroline took the following day off from work to pack her things at the apartment she used to share with Clay. She walked through the door and nearly jumped ten feet when she saw him at the table.

"I didn't think you'd be here, Clay. I'm sorry, I can come back later or something," Caroline offered.

"No. I wanted to be here." Clay's eyelids were swollen and dark circles surrounded his eyes.

"Are you sure? I promise I won't take anything that isn't mine." She glanced around at the things they shared.

Clay tried to laugh, "I don't think you're going to take my stuff Caroline. I just..." He stopped talking and placed a finger against the side of his head. "It just doesn't make sense, Care."

Caroline's heart started to throb in her chest. She moved to put her purse on the counter. "What do you mean?" she asked as calmly as possible.

"I still don't get why you rushed off to New York? If Tracey's fine, then why'd you leave like that? I don't understand where you went." Clay's eyes crinkled as he waited.

She felt horrible for lying and knew she needed to come clean. At first, she thought the lie was to protect Clay from being hurt more. But the reality was, she was protecting herself. She didn't want to give Clay a reason to hate her.

Caroline wondered if she had the courage to be completely honest with him. She looked at Clay's somber face before he implored, "Please...just tell me the truth."

Nerves rattled her body from the inside out. "I got a phone call during the party." Caroline moved to sit in the chair directly across from him. She swallowed hard, the lump noticeable in her throat. "Do you remember the guy from the airplane?"

Clay's forehead wrinkled. "Jackson, or something like that?"

Caroline nodded. "He was in a real bad accident."

"So? What does that have to do with you?"

As Caroline gazed at the table in front of her, Clay's anger returned. "Caroline! What does that guy getting in an accident have to do with you?"

Caroline sobbed uncontrollably.

"Caroline! Answer me!" he shouted at her. She looked up at him as the confusion in his eyes subsided. He rose from the table, grabbed the chair he sat on and hurled it into the wall behind him. "Are you kidding me? That guy? Have you been talking to him all this time?"

Caroline felt her stomach twist into tightly bound knots. Her face drained of all color as she fought off the urge to throw up. "Have you been cheating on me?" Clay demanded, his body trembling with angry thoughts.

"No! I didn't cheat on you. I promise!" She finally spoke, but her words offered little comfort.

"I don't believe you!" he screamed at her, the veins in his neck bulging with every beat of his adrenaline-filled heart.

"I swear, Clay. I never did anything with him."

He pounded his fists on top of the table with such force that the glasses and candle crashed onto their sides. His breaths were quick and heavy as tiny beads of sweat rolled down the side of his beet red face. His hands clenched into fists and then unclenched, his knuckles shifting between white and pink. He turned to pace around the living room as Caroline watched him helplessly, her body wracked with uncertainty.

Clay closed his mouth and tried to breathe calmly, his breath rushing loudly through his nostrils. He walked over to the tossed chair that had punctured a small hole in the wall and picked it up. He brought it to the table and sat down. "Tell me everything," he insisted through clenched teeth.

Caroline wiped the tears from her face, scared to death to admit the whole truth to him. "What do you want to know?"

"How many times have you seen him?" Clay shouted.

"I had lunch with him once after the flight, but that's it," she said, her voice shaking.

"Did you kiss him?" Clay asked coldly.

Caroline suddenly felt like she was on trial. "No."

"How often do the two of you talk?"

She thought back at the past year. "Um, at first we talked a lot."

Clay interrupted. "Every day?"

Caroline nodded. "Pretty much."

"Go on," Clay insisted. "Did you talk on the phone, Facebook, email, what?"

Caroline wanted this to stop, but Clay deserved answers, no matter how hard they were for her to admit. Her bottom lip quivered. "We talked on the phone sometimes. We sent texts mostly."

"When?" Clay asked impatiently.

"When what?"

"When did you talk on the phone? At work? Here?" His tone filled with disgust.

"Um..." Caroline stumbled and focused on her trembling hands. "Here, mostly."

"Where was I?" He glared.

"You were at work, Clay. You're always at work," she commented.

Clay gave a quick laugh. "Oh. So this is my fault, right? Because I was never around? Always at work?"

"No! That's just when we talked. You were at work and I was here."

Clay's guilt got the better of him momentarily and his voice softened. "Did this happen because I was never home?"

Caroline recoiled. "No. Clay…this was never about you being home, or not being home. It wouldn't have mattered if you were here every second of every day."

"Then why did it happen? It doesn't make sense. Nothing makes sense." Clay buried his face into his hands.

"I don't know. I thought I was perfectly happy," she admitted.

"But obviously you weren't. Whether you realize it or not, something was missing for you," Clay pointed out.

"I don't know if I believe that. I don't know what I believe any more." She struggled to push her overwhelming guilt aside and take the blame.

Clay replayed her words in his mind. His voice raged. "So then, what happened? You said *at first* you talked a lot…then what?"

The rollercoaster of his emotions made Caroline cringe. She looked at Clay and tried to smile. "We got engaged."

He shrugged. "And…you suddenly grew a conscience and stopped talking to him?"

"No." The pounding of her heart hammered in her ears. "He stopped talking to me."

"Aw, what a stand-up guy." Clay applauded mockingly.

"Stop. Please. I've hurt so many people, I can't take it any more." Her insides felt like they had shattered into irreparable fragments.

He eyeballed her, his lips pressed tightly together. "I just have one more question Caroline and then I'll stop," he promised.

"Okay." A sigh escaped from her lips.

"See, if I've got this all right…you got a phone call." Clay counted on his fingers. "And you left me alone at our engagement party without saying a word…you flew across the country to be with some guy you barely know…and now you're breaking off our engagement and moving out."

Caroline tried to catch her breath when the sobs choked at her throat. She closed her eyes tightly and fought to control her emotions.

Clay continued, his voice void of any emotion. "So I can only come to one conclusion." Caroline peered nervously at him, her face streaked with tears. "You must love him." He scowled and she hated herself in that moment for what she'd done to him. "So do you? Do you love this guy?"

Tears continued to pour out as she kept quiet, unsure of what to say.

"Answer me, Caroline!" he demanded. "You owe me at least that much."

"I don't know," she lied.

"At least give me enough respect to tell me to my face." His fist slammed against the table and Caroline jumped.

She answered through short, rapid breaths. "You're right. I'm sorry. Yes." She tried to steady her breathing. "Yes, I love him."

"Get out."

"But…" Her face twisted in agony as her eyes pleaded with Clay to understand.

His chest heaved under his shirt. "Get out. Get your stuff another time. I need you to leave. Now." He glared at her, hatred filled his watery eyes.

Caroline rose from the table, grabbed her purse, and ran out the door. She flung herself into the black iron railing and peered down at the ground, three stories below. She panted as tears fell from her face. She followed the marble stairs down one floor before she crumbled to the ground, desperate to release the pain. If there was ever a day she felt worse in her life, she wasn't sure she could pinpoint it.

Of course getting the news about Jackson had forced her to experience agony on a level she never knew existed. Every single breath physically hurt to breathe. Jackson's accident filled her with regret, sorrow, and worry. She was terrified that Jackson might die and that fear overwhelmed her constantly. It was the kind of pain that made her whole world violently crash in around her.

She explained it to Bailey once. *"It's like looking into a full-length mirror and seeing nothing but pure beauty in the reflection…and then watching helplessly as it shatters into a thousand pieces before your eyes, knowing that you can do nothing to keep it from breaking…"*

But this was different.

The pain and heartbreak that currently ensued with Clay was completely within her control. She was solely responsible. No matter how right the decision was for her, nothing could ease the torment of hurting another.

And it wasn't like she didn't love Clay. She did. He was everything she had ever wanted in life, until Jackson came along and screwed it all up. Now she broke off her engagement and ended the chapter she assumed was going to be her whole book. It hurt to walk away from a relationship that wasn't flawed, imperfect, or unhealthy. It hurt to leave something so comfortable.

Once her heart felt steady, she started down the rest of the stairs and fumbled through her purse for her phone. She dialed Bailey's number at work.

"Packed already?" Bailey asked without even saying *hello*.

"No. Clay was waiting for me. I told him about Jackson."

"You did WHAT?" Bailey yelled.

"He asked! I couldn't lie."

"So what happened?" Bailey whispered loudly.

"I've never seen him so mad," Caroline confessed as she tried unsuccessfully to block the image from her memory.

"Really? That's kinda hot."

"Bays."

"Sorry, it's just I didn't think the guy had it in him. He's always so composed all the time."

Caroline let out an annoyed breath. "Great. Can we discuss your appreciation for Clay's anger later?"

"Definitely. So wait, did you get your stuff or not?"

"That's why I'm calling. He kicked me out before I could get anything," Caroline answered, clearly flustered.

Bailey stifled a laugh. "Shut UP! That guy's full of surprises!"

"BAILEY!" Caroline screamed into the phone.

"Calm down," Bailey hissed. "I'll go over there after work and get your stuff. He won't even think about pulling any of that crap with me."

"Thank you."

"You're welcome." Bailey went to hang up and then remembered. "Hey, any news on Jackson?"

"I haven't heard anything," sighed Caroline.

"No news is good news, right?"

"Sure." Caroline hung up before Bailey could ask her any more questions. She wandered bleary-eyed up and down a few streets before she realized she had no idea where she was.

♡ Eighteen

Eight weeks had passed since Caroline had last seen Jackson. Alex had called two days earlier to let her know that the swelling in his brain had subsided and the doctors were going to try to bring him out of the coma. There was little that he could guarantee, but he promised to let her know when Jackson opened his eyes.

"Are you gonna go out there or what?" Bailey asked.

"I can't. I felt so out of place when I was there before. His best friend hates me, he has another girlfriend, and his parents didn't even know who I was."

"So what?" Bailey snapped.

"What if he doesn't want me? I left him that letter. If I'm what he wants, then I know he'll call. But if he doesn't, then I have my answer."

"You infuriate me, you know?" Bailey's comment made Caroline chuckle. "I'm serious," Bailey continued. "Leaving your future in the hands of a letter? A letter you handed to another *girl*, Caroline Weber! If that was me, I'd have thrown that letter in the trash the second you walked out the door. Pshhh…letter, my ass."

Caroline paused. "She wouldn't do that."

Bailey groaned. "How do you know? You don't even know that girl. She doesn't owe you anything."

"Don't worry. Alex knows about the letter too."

"Well, thank God! You could have told me that in the first place," Bailey chastised.

"I'm heading home. You coming?"

"Not yet. I still have to finish some stuff first. I'll see you there." Bailey sat in her cubicle and typed furiously.

Caroline headed toward the local deli to grab a sandwich before they closed. She squinted as she saw a couple headed toward her. Was that Clay? Her feet stopped. She was certain it was him. Walking with another girl? Was that his girlfriend? Had he moved on already?

Caroline chastised herself. It wasn't any of her business. She had given up all rights to know about Clay's personal life when she decided not to be a part of it. She continued walking, each step bringing her closer to him. Clay's pace slowed to a stop and Caroline did the same.

"Hi, Care," Clay's voice wavered. "Uh, this is Gina. We work together."

Caroline reached out and shook the pretty girl's hand. "It's nice to meet you, Gina."

"It's nice to meet you, too." Gina smiled and turned to face Clay, "I'll give you some time alone." She squeezed Clay's shoulder before walking toward a corner store.

Caroline did her best to play the uncaring, totally-over-it ex-girlfriend—um, ex-fiancée—but this was harder than she ever would have thought. Her chest felt tight as jealousy filled her every pore. She knew that logically she didn't want Clay back, but the truth was that she didn't want to see him with anyone else either. She felt irrational and immature.

"It's good to see you," Clay said.

Caroline swallowed hard. "You too. Gina seems nice and she's really pretty." Caroline forced a smile.

"She is nice. We're just friends, though." Clay insisted as he looked in Gina's direction. "She's just really been there for me, you know?"

"That's great…" Caroline fought to hold back her jealousy, "that you have someone to talk to about everything."

Clay cringed and then asked, "So, how's Jackson? Any change in his condition?"

Caroline's eyes widened with surprise. "No. They aren't sure he'll wake up. And if he does, there's no guarantee that he'll be the same." She fought to hold back the tears that formed.

He reached out his hand and put it on her shoulder. "I'm sure he will. He'll be okay."

Caroline knew Clay didn't have to say that. He didn't have to ask about Jackson. Hell, he didn't even have to stop and talk to her at all.

"Thanks," she said, as she looked down at the ground. "I'm really sorry about everything, Clay. Truly I am. I never meant to hurt you." Her eyes met his.

Clay nodded. "I know. I've done a lot of thinking these past couple of months. You know, I never should have proposed to you that night anyway."

"What do you mean?" she asked, her eyes wide with surprise.

"I just mean…" He arched his eyebrows while he thought for a moment. "I did it for all the wrong reasons. I mean, I knew something was *off* between us. And instead of trying to figure out what it was, I just tried to fix it."

He shrugged his shoulders. "I thought proposing would solve everything and make whatever it was that was wrong…*right*. I thought it would instantly make you happy again."

Caroline refused to let Clay shoulder any blame. "But I should have talked to you. I should have told you what was going on with me. I should have been honest, but I was too busy trying to fight off everything I was feeling. I tried to pretend that I was okay, when I wasn't."

"But I knew you weren't okay. And I didn't even try to talk to you about it. In all honesty, you were the last person I ever worried about losing or falling apart. I feel like I took you for granted." His head shook.

"You'd never had a reason to worry before. This thing with Jackson…it was beyond any of our control. I know it sounds stupid, but it was never about you and me. I knew how much you loved me, Clay, and I never felt taken for granted." She longed for her truth to comfort him.

"Thank you," Clay responded, his mouth unsmiling and his gaze sincere.

"I mean it. I really am sorry." The pain she caused still burdened her.

"I know you are." Clay shifted his weight. "Look, Care, I used to want to make you hurt just as badly as I did. But now that feels like a long time ago. I don't want you to be upset any more. I really am okay. And I want you to be, too."

She was happily surprised when he leaned in to hug her. Her body warmed in his familiar arms as she spoke gently in his ear. "Thank you so much. I wish you the best in everything. You truly deserve it."

Clay smiled and as Caroline started to walk away, she heard him call her name. Her stomach dipped as she turned to face him. "I forgive you." He looked at his feet and then back up into her eyes. "I think I understand why you did what you did."

It was as if an SUV lifted off of her shoulders and the blame she carried shattered to the ground at her feet. She almost fell to the sidewalk in relief, but braced herself against a cement parking meter. "Thank you, Clay," she answered

through her tears as she watched him continue down the
street with Gina at his side.

Her body felt light and each breath filled her with relief.
She hadn't realized the extent of the guilt she had been
carrying until it fell free from her. She had lived with it for so
long that it had become a part of her. In hoping that her
words could help him heal, he had just given her the ultimate
gift...the gift of forgiveness.

♡ N i n e t e e n

When Jackson first opened his eyes, all he could make out were blurry shapes and patches of light and dark. The shapes slowly turned into blurry images and he could distinguish the faces of his parents…then Sally, Tommy, and Alex. He tried to smile, but his mouth felt like he had just left the dentist's office.

****

Alex and Tommy stood in the back of the room as Jackson's parents were briefed; Sally hovered nearby. The doctor was encouraging as she spoke to his parents. "Jackson is responding more quickly than we expected after reducing his medication. It will be a few days before we can determine the extent of the damage, though." She went on, "Jackson will need extensive physical therapy to regain basic motor functions. There is the possibility of speech therapy, as well."

Alex high-fived Sally and Tommy at the news and congratulations were exchanged all around. Jackson's friends didn't know what the future held for him, but one thing was certain—he would get to have one.

****

Caroline received a call at work with the good news. "Hey, Caroline, it's Alex!"

At first, her heart stopped when she saw Alex's name on her caller ID, but the tone of his voice immediately erased any concerns she had about the call bearing bad news. "Hi! What's up? How are you?"

"I'm great! I just wanted you to know that he opened his eyes."

Caroline's grin stretched from ear to ear. "Really? When?"

"About ten minutes ago."

"Oh my gosh, that's awesome!" she exclaimed. "That *is* awesome...right?" she asked.

Alex laughed and then explained. "It's definitely awesome. But, he can't talk yet and the doctors aren't sure when his speech will come back, or to what extent. I just wanted you to know that he's awake."

"Thank you so much, Alex. I really appreciate the updates."

"Of course. I'll call you if anything else happens, okay?" he said.

"Okay," Caroline said one last time before she hung up. Her hopes high, she figured it was only a matter of time before her phone would ring with Jackson's voice on the other end.

She turned towards Bailey's cubicle and beamed in her direction. "He's awake!" she shouted in a loud whisper.

Bailey looked up from her work and squealed. "Really? How do you know? Did he call?"

"One sec." Caroline held up a finger, then she thumbed Tracey a text message with the news. Tracey responded right back telling her "*Great news!*" and asked when she was "*Coming back out?*"

Caroline turned back to Bailey. "Alex called. He said that Jackson couldn't talk yet, but his eyes were open."

"That's great news, Care. Let's go out and celebrate tonight!"

"Sounds great." Caroline could use some fun in her life. She had been all but consumed in thoughts of Jackson for what felt like forever. And she'd been doing a lot of waiting—waiting for Jackson to wake up, waiting for him to call, and waiting for her life to begin again.

The girls headed straight to a restaurant and bar after work. Caroline was still on cloud nine from Alex's call that afternoon. They sat in a small booth and Caroline ordered appetizers and a light beer.

"So, how long until Jackson calls, you think?" Bailey asked.

"I don't know. I mean, Alex said he couldn't talk yet. But..." Caroline's voice trailed off.

"But what?" Bailey rolled her eyes. "Oh, don't *even*, Caroline."

"Don't even what?"

"You think he's not gonna call. I can't believe I'm best friends with an idiot."

Caroline shook her head with a laugh. "No. I think it's idiotic to *assume* he will."

Bailey slapped the table and Caroline grabbed her drink before it toppled over. "Ugh. Really? Of course he's going to call. He loves you. Even Alex said so!"

"Alex also thought Jackson's parents knew who I was. So, he could be wrong."

Bailey shrugged; Caroline was right about that. Alex had been just as surprised as Caroline when they realized that Jackson's parents didn't know who she was. "I still think he'll call," Bailey said with optimism.

Caroline smiled. "I hope so."

"There's no way this all happened for nothing. All the drama, the heartache, leaving Clay…"

"You better be right," Caroline said.

"Dur. Of course I'm right. I'm smart, remember?" Bailey laughed, and held up her glass.

♡ Twenty

The days seemed to pass in slow motion as Caroline waited for the call that never came. She attempted to fill the agony of waiting during the day with work and let Bailey drag her out at night.

She sat at her desk trying to concentrate on the ad mock-up that was due before the end of the day, but Jackson consumed her every thought. Caroline wanted to believe that he would call soon, but worried his silence meant what she had feared the most…that Jackson had really moved on and was no longer in love with her.

Caroline silently berated herself for the hundredth time for waiting so long to walk away from Clay. She had finally admitted what she had felt since that first day, but it was apparently too late and she had no one to blame but herself. She had waited too long…treated him badly…abused his heart. She snapped her laptop shut in frustration, picked up her cell phone and checked to make sure she still had a signal. She did.

Bailey walked by her desk quickly without stopping. "Anything yet?"

Caroline simply shook her head and Bailey mouthed, *"I'm sorry"* as she continued on to the conference room.

****

Jackson laughed in his hospital bed as Sally told him about a funny incident at the bar. Alex leaned in the doorway and watched Sally's interaction with Jackson. He had tried to be patient, wanting to ask his best friend about Caroline, but once again it seemed like a bad time. Sally was always in Jackson's room whenever Alex dropped in, and he didn't want to hurt her feelings.

When Jackson first awoke, he couldn't speak clearly and had been in intense physical and speech therapy ever since. Sally made a point to be at the hospital as much as possible, and Alex knew that her support had been good for Jackson.

Jackson joked with Sally like old times, and Alex smiled in relief at the improvement he noticed. His friend was more and more like his old self every day. Maybe there was no time like the present.

"So…" Alex ventured. "How are things with Caroline?" Sally stiffened and leaned back slightly.

Jackson's brows furrowed and he dropped Sally's hand. "What do you mean?"

"Haven't you talked to her?" Alex asked pointedly.

"No. Why would I?"

"She was here, you know." Alex glanced at Sally. "You *did* know she was here, right?"

Jackson started fidgeting in his bed. "No, I didn't. How would I know that if no one told me? When was she here?"

"When you first got into the accident...she came to the hospital."

"She came here? She flew...out here?" Jackson's face froze and his eyes were unfocused as he obviously struggled to understand.

"Yeah, I thought you knew that." Alex shrugged.

"How the hell would I know that?" Jackson shouted, his color rising as his temper flared.

"Because she left you a letter!" Alex retorted.

"What letter?" he asked in disbelief..

Alex looked in Sally's direction. "Sal, you never gave him the letter?"-

****

An agitated heat swirled throughout Jackson's body. None of this made sense......could Caroline have really come to the hospital? He didn't remember any of it. He frowned at Sally, whose face had turned pale. Slowly, she picked up her purse and pulled out the tattered envelope that had "Jackson" written on the front in blue ink.

"I'm sorry. I should have given this to you weeks ago." Her hands quivered as she handed Jackson the envelope.

"You've had a letter from Caroline this whole time?" Jackson asked, his voice dangerously soft. "You kept it from me?"

"I'm so sorry, Jackson. I was supposed to give it to you when you woke up, but I panicked." Sally shifted in her chair and pulled her purse closer to her body. She glanced up at Alex for support, but he looked away.

"You panicked? You knew how I felt about her." Jackson struggled to keep his temper in check as his voice rose and his face flushed with color.

Sally stuttered, her voice shaking. "It just happened so fast after you woke up. For the first time, you actually needed me. And I didn't want to lose that…I didn't want to lose you." She reached out to touch his arm, but drew back as he stiffened.

Sally leaned against the wall and closed her eyes. "But I realize now that I never truly had you in the first place, so you can't lose something you don't have, right?"

Jackson refused to look at her. Without a word he yanked the envelope from Sally's hand and opened it carefully. He unfolded the piece of paper and read it to himself.

Dear Jackson,

You once told me that we were like two ships passing in the night…that we had found each other, but couldn't be together because there were forces, situations, or other things that we couldn't overcome. And for a long time, I believed the words that you wrote to me. I had to. I knew that what we'd found in one another was truly rare, but I held on to the notion that we simply weren't meant to be. As painful as that notion was, I chose to accept it the same way you had.

But now, as I sit in the hospital where you lie helplessly in a room down the hall, I wonder if they weren't so much situations we couldn't overcome, as much as situations we chose not to. And by we, I really mean me.

I sit here unsure of your feelings for me and I think I finally understand how you must have felt all along. And I can never apologize enough for the pain I caused you. As hard as it was for me, I know it was harder for you. And for that, I am truly sorry.

It took almost losing you for me to see that there is no one else I want to be with other than you. There's nothing more I'd rather do than sit in that room by your side every moment until you open those beautiful blue eyes and look at me again, but I'm not naïve enough to think that your life hasn't continued on without me (Sally is fantastic by the way). I don't want to assume that I still hold a place in your world. But if I do…and if you still want to be with me the way I desperately know I want to be with you…then call me when you wake up and I'll be on the next flight out.

I love you…I always have. I was just too stupid, or cautious, or filled with worry and guilt to do anything about it. I'm finally ready to follow my heart—and all roads lead to your door.

xoxo, Caroline

"I can't believe you kept this from me." Jackson said tightly, his gaze focused on the letter he couldn't believe he was holding in his hands.

"I'll make it right with her. I'll do anything. Please, just forgive me," Sally pleaded.

Jackson shook his head and looked at Alex. "Does she know I'm awake?"

"I called her the day you woke up."

"Of course you did," Tommy chimed in snidely from the hallway.

Alex turned to glance behind him. "When did you get here?"

"Just now."

Jackson ignored their exchange as he quickly calculated the number of days he'd been awake. He read her letter one more time before cursing under his breath. "She thinks I don't love her."

"Why would you say that?" Alex asked.

"Because she told me to call her when I woke up if I still wanted to be with her," Jackson explained, holding up the letter.

Alex's face dropped. "Oh."

"Alex, I've been out of the coma for *weeks*, and she knows that."

"But…"

Jackson interjected, "Have I mentioned the fact that I haven't called her?"

"Unbelievable," Tommy snarled and stormed out.

"But you can fix it! Just one phone call will fix everything. She'll understand. Call her!" Alex pleaded.

"I can't." Jackson sighed as his eyes glazed over.

"What do you mean, you can't?"

"Did he meet her when she was here?" Jackson tilted his head in Tommy's direction.

Alex snorted. "Oh yeah. He met her, all right."

"Was he mean to her?" he asked through clenched teeth.

"That's an understatement."

"What's his problem?"

Alex shrugged his shoulders. "I honestly don't know."

"I think I do," Sally offered softly. She looked over at Jackson before he nodded with silent approval for her to continue.

"It's hard to stand by and watch your best friend go down a road you know will end badly for them," she began. "It's like you see them in the path of an oncoming train, but they don't see anything past the pretty trees near the tracks. You want to push them out of the way so they don't get run over, but they refuse to move. So you're forced to stand there helplessly and watch the devastation happen, powerless to do anything to stop it."

"I guess." Jackson conceded. "But I'm a big boy; I can take care of myself. It's my decision if I want to stand on the train tracks or not. I know what's coming, but it's my risk to take."

"It's still painful to watch."

All heads turned at Tommy's comment. Alex wasn't sure if he was more surprised that Tommy had returned, or by what he had said.

"But I didn't ask you to watch," Jackson argued.

"But as your friend, I can't help it," Tommy insisted. "I can't just walk away and pretend I don't care. It just sucked, okay? I've never seen you like this about a girl." Tommy eyeballed Sally.

"Sorry, Sal," he continued, "but it's true. Jax, you were crazy for this girl. But she had a boyfriend and I couldn't help but think that you were headed for some serious heartbreak. Not to mention the fact that the whole situation was pretty messed up."

"You're a good friend, Tommy," Jackson acknowledged. "And I appreciate your concern, but you have to let me live my own life. I knew that I was heading in a potentially bad place. But I had to take that chance." His eyes softened and he smiled at the thought of Caroline. "See, she was worth the risk. You can't make those decisions for me."

Tommy took a deep breath. "I know that. It's just still hard to stand idly by and watch you get hurt."

"Are *you* in love with me?" Jackson asked sarcastically and the whole room burst into laughter.

"I'd punch the shit out of you right now, if you weren't lying in a hospital bed," Tommy promised.

"Lucky me," Jackson smiled.

"I don't mean to break up the 'bromance' we have going on, but..." Alex paused and smiled. "Are you gonna call the girl, or what?"

Jackson took a deep breath. "I have to think."

"What is there to think about, Jax?" Alex prodded.

"I just need to figure some stuff out, okay?" Jackson snapped harshly and Alex shut up.

Sally watched the exchange between the guys and suddenly felt out of place being there. "Can you guys give us a moment alone?" she asked meekly. Tommy and Alex exchanged glances, then slipped out the door and closed it behind them.

She sat up a little straighter and folded her hands tightly in her lap, before she took a deep breath and looked Jackson directly in the eye. "Jackson, I truly am sorry."

His face softened and he reached for her hand. "I know. I don't think what you did was right, but I know where it came from." Jackson regretted that he had never been able to return Sally's feelings for him, and his voice gentled. "I need to thank you," he said, catching her off guard.

"Thank me...for what?" she stammered.

"For loving me," he said kindly, and squeezed her hand. "I know it hasn't been easy for you, knowing that my heart was unavailable. But you never let that stop you from taking care of me this whole time. I know you haven't left my side for a single day."

Sally's face flushed and her eyes welled with tears. "I didn't want to."

Jackson smiled. "I know. You're an amazingly kind and giving woman. One day you'll find the right guy for you. And if he treats you the way I did, I'll beat the crap out of him."

Sally wiped at her eyes and laughed. "Thanks, Jackson. And Caroline's incredible, by the way. She truly is."

"You liked her?" His face brightened and Sally could see that he wanted to ask more.

"I *do* like her. It took about all of five minutes for me to see what you saw in her," Sally admitted.

Jackson kissed the back of her hand and looked into her eyes.

Sally grabbed her purse and stood to leave. "Thank you for showing me what I've been missing," she said, and leaned over to kiss Jackson's cheek.

Jackson watched Sally walk out the door and knew with certainty that she wouldn't return. Now he needed to figure out what to do about Caroline. Of course he wanted to be with her, but it had been weeks since he'd woken up. What if in his hesitation to call her, she had gone back to Clay? What if she had moved on? What if she were mad at him? His mind raced through a million different thoughts, but he didn't pick up the phone.

When his head began to ache from his never-ending brain chatter, Jackson forced himself to sleep. He decided to call Caroline the following day and hoped she would understand and still want to see him.

****

Jackson watched as a figure approached in the distance. He put his hand up to block the setting sun and knew immediately that it was *her*. Caroline walked quickly through the tall grass and flowers toward him. As she came closer, he saw the huge smile on her face. He ran to her, but stopped short of picking her up and swinging her around. Instead, he paused and looked her up and down, noting that she was wearing one of his white button-down shirts. He wondered briefly how she got it, but then quickly dismissed the thought.

Jackson looked at her feet. "Nice boots."

Caroline smiled. "I guess I could have picked better shoes to walk in."

Jackson's face dropped. "You walked here?"

"Of course," Caroline responded, as if his question were completely absurd.

"From *California*?"

"How else would I get here, silly?"

****

Jackson opened his eyes and looked around the hospital room. Alex sat in the corner thumbing his phone when Jackson started to laugh.

Alex looked up. "What are you laughing at?"

Jackson shook his head. "I just had the craziest dream."

"Caroline?"

"Oh yeah. But you should have seen her. And she said she walked here from California, like there was no other possible way she could have gotten here." Jackson cracked up.

"So are you going to call her or what?" Alex pushed.

Jackson checked the clock on the wall. "It's too early there. It's only six in the morning."

"So?"

"I don't want to wake her up. She likes to sleep in," Jackson said with a smile.

"I don't think she'd mind," Alex noted.

"I'm going to wait until after she gets off work. I don't want to have this phone call before she goes, or while she's at the office. I think it's best to wait until the end of her day," Jackson said with confidence.

"The end of whose day?" A female voice caught both Alex and Jackson by surprise. Caroline walked through the door wearing jeans and a white tank top, followed closely by Tommy, whose grin spoke volumes.

Jackson's eyes lit up and he fidgeted in the bed. "Caroline…"

"Hi." Her face beamed.

"How'd you…what are you…" Jackson looked from her to Tommy, his brows raised.

Caroline eyed Tommy. "Tommy called and told me everything. I got on the next flight."

Alex stepped over and punched Tommy in the arm. "Softie."

Tommy's smile quickly faded, a scowl in its place. "I will hurt you."

Alex grinned from ear to ear. "We'll give you two some time alone." Alex grabbed Tommy by the sleeve and pulled him out of the room.

Caroline's heart beat fiercely as she met Jackson's gaze.

Jackson focused on her, and held out his hand. "Get over here."

She practically ran to his side. Her body trembled with anticipation as Jackson grabbed the back of her neck and pulled her down toward him. He kissed her softly at first, his lips tender and gentle. Passion quickly erupted, as months of wanting and waiting exploded with intensity. Their mouths and tongues explored one another with a ferocious longing. Electricity swirled around them as the energy of their souls collided.

Jackson pulled his head back and opened his eyes as if to reassure himself that she was really there…and not another dream. He watched as Caroline slowly opened her eyes and smiled.

She found herself craving more of him, as if she could no longer exist without the warmth of his touch. The way his lips felt and the taste of his tongue simmered with blissful satisfaction in the recesses of her mind. She dove toward him, crushing her lips against his as desire took over.

His grip loosened and she found herself breathless. Her feet tingled and pricked as their energies mingled. Her finger traced along his cheek as he admired her.

"I love you, Caroline Weber."

Like a balloon floating toward the sky, no longer tied down, she felt her heart soar inside her. "I've waited so long to hear that."

"I did tell you once before, you know," he reminded her.

"Yeah, but this time I don't feel guilty. Or bad about loving you back."

He raised an eyebrow. "Oh, so you love me?"

"You know I do."

"Say it."

"I love you, Jackson Parks."

"It's about time." He brushed at her hair and traced her bottom lip with his thumb. "Now stop talking." He pulled her close and his mouth found hers, hungry with desire.

"I'm never going to get tired of doing that." Jackson's eyes turned dark and he held her tightly.

"I'm counting on it," Caroline replied, her grip on him equally as strong.

Their mouths came together again, pulled in by some unexplainable force. Driven by desire, lust, and passion, they lost themselves in each another, content to finally be together, where they belonged.

♡ Twenty-One

Six Weeks Later...

"I can't believe you're really leaving." Bailey pouted from the couch.

Caroline sat on the floor and continued to wrap her framed photos, nestling them carefully in the open cardboard box in front of her. "Yes, you can," she said, without looking up.

Bailey chuckled. "Yeah. I can."

Bailey's living room was crowded with stacks of boxes and suitcases, all filled with Caroline's belongings. Only a few boxes remained unsealed, and Caroline crouched in front of one, tucking in the last item before she picked up her tape gun to seal it closed.

"It's funny how things work out, huh?" Bailey picked up a sweatshirt from the pile of clothing on the couch, folded it, and handed it down to Caroline.

"How do you mean?" Caroline asked as she leaned over the box.

"Well, for starters, Mr. Walters is letting you transfer to the New York office, so you already have a kick-ass job." Bailey's face screamed "You're Welcome" as she continued. "And...one of your best friends lives in the city, so you already have a place to live..."

"All true," Caroline cut in.

Bailey's eyes narrowed impatiently. "Hey! I wasn't done yet!"

Caroline leaned back and threw her hands up in the air. "Whoa."

Bailey cleared her throat. "As I was saying…kick-ass job, place to live, oh yeah, did I mention the boyfriend?"

"Uh, no. I don't think you did. Is there one?" Caroline teased. The word *boyfriend* conjured up images of Jackson's eyes in Caroline's mind and she suddenly felt as though she was drowning in a sea of blue…only she didn't mind.

Bailey brought her finger to her lips and bit at it seductively. "Ooooh, is there ever."

Caroline burst out laughing. "You're such a nut! This is why I love you."

"It's funny how things fall into place when you're on the right path." Bailey's eyes twinkled with delight and Caroline's entire face was aglow. "Remind me again why you're not moving in with Jackson?" Bailey picked up a pair of jeans and aligned the legs before folding them.

When a chuckle came out mixed with an exasperated breath, Caroline coughed. "I've told you this, like what? A million times already?"

Bailey huffed. "Just tell me once more."

"You writing a book or something?"

"Ha! You wish. Just tell me why, after everything that has happened between the two of you, you aren't seizing every moment like it could be your last?"

"I didn't want to rush things."

Bailey handed down the jeans. "Didn't want to rush things? Why should you? I mean, you only called off your wedding for the guy...and he only almost died."

Caroline grabbed the jeans and smacked Bailey's arm with them. "Shut up. Seriously, this is a huge step. I just want to be smart about it."

"No, you're right, he'll probably be sick of you in a week anyway."

"You're pretty much the worst friend ever."

"Yay right! You know I'm kidding." Bailey nudged Caroline's ribs with her foot.

"I know. But that thought does linger in the back of my mind," Caroline admitted.

"What thought? That he'll get sick of you?"

"Not that, necessarily. But what if it doesn't work out between us?"

"Do you really think it won't?" Bailey asked with surprise.

"No, but you never know. I mean, things happened really fast since his accident. I don't want to be careless. So until we're sure, I'm living with Tracey."

"Makes sense." Bailey nodded with approval.

Caroline folded the last box top and ran tape across it before wiping the dust off her hands on the leg of her jeans. "All done."

"Should we start loading them into your car?"

"Yeah. We need to get on the road soon." Caroline glanced at her watch.

"Will it really take us six whole days to get there?" Bailey whined and let out an annoyed breath.

"I don't know," Caroline admitted. "I've never driven to New York from San Francisco before."

"I was just asking, jeez."

"I swear if you annoy me, I will ditch your ass in the middle of Nebraska or something," Caroline warned, wagging her finger.

"You will do nothing of the sort or so help me God, I will *hunt.you.down*," Bailey threatened.

"You'd have to catch me first," Caroline challenged and tossed the box she was holding at Bailey.

The cell phone's ring broke up the horseplay. Caroline scrambled around desperately trying to locate the sound until Bailey pointed toward the couch. Caroline dived over the couch and pulled the cell phone out from under a throw pillow.

"Hey, Tray." Caroline raised her eyebrows as Bailey waved *hi* and grabbed a box. "We're just packing up the car now and then we'll be on our way." Caroline nodded her head against the phone. "Yep. I know. I can't wait! I'm so excited!" A smile spread across her face. "Thank you so much for letting me stay with you. I know, it's just…I know. I love you too. See you soon!"

"We should go," Bailey reminded her, pointing at her watch.

With one last long, deep breath, Caroline tossed her blue duffle bag's strap over her shoulder and reached for her brown leather suitcase. Bailey held the last two boxes as they turned for the door.

Caroline paused in the doorway to look around the old apartment one last time. Her eyes followed the walls down the hallway and stopped on the photographs that hung there, sans frames. She saw an old photograph of herself and Bailey from high school that made her smile.

"Goodbye, San Francisco," she whispered as excitement flowed through her. She longed to see Jackson's face and couldn't wait to be back in New York City.

"Let's go already!" Bailey's voice echoed in the stairwell outside the apartment door.

Caroline turned, her heart racing with anticipation, and headed out the door.

Epilogue

Caroline was lost in thought. She could hardly believe it had been three years. It seemed like ages ago…like when she tried to remember her life before Jackson. Of course she remembered everything, but the memories didn't hold the same feelings any more. The drama, the hurt, and the pain she had caused…were all now deeply rooted in the past, a past so distant that it almost felt like another lifetime.

The last Caroline had heard, Clay was rapidly moving up the corporate ladder and was doing well. Apparently, he had recently proposed to his co-worker, Gina. Caroline smiled to herself, thankful that Clay had finally been able to find happiness.

She looked at her reflection in the antique mirror that hung on the dark wall and adjusted wisps of her hair one last time. In the mirror, she saw the reflections of Tracey and Bailey smiling from ear to ear. She grinned back at her two best friends, and thought about how stunning they both looked in their knee-length black cocktail dresses, remembering the fun and silliness that they'd shared while shopping for them. Caroline stood up, adjusted the layers of her long white gown, and walked toward her bridesmaids. She slipped an arm around each of them, wanting to give them each one last hug before the ceremony began.

"You look beautiful, Care," Tracey said, her eyes brimming with tears.

"Not as pretty as us, but you're a close second." Bailey winked.

Caroline laughed. "Well, we can't all be the super hot bridesmaids...someone has to be the bride."

Caroline glanced down at the ring on her left hand. A stunning, heart-shaped diamond nestled inside her fiancé's design. Her heart fluttered against her rib cage with excitement and joy.

"Better you than me—that's for sure." Bailey elbowed Tracey. "Right, Tracey?"

Tracey picked up a tissue and leaned toward the mirror, dabbing at her eyes. "Oh definitely. *I* don't want to marry Jackson."

"Hey!" Caroline frowned for a second, then laughed.

Tracey turned and brushed Caroline's veil from her shoulder. "Are you ready to do this?" she asked.

Caroline's face brightened. "I can't wait to do this!"

Bailey handed Caroline a bouquet of white tulips and opened the large wooden door. She peeked out and called, "She's in here, Mr. W," and Caroline's father stepped in and gently took his daughter's hand.

As the music began to play, Tracey and Bailey walked slowly into the sunlight, while Caroline waited patiently behind. Tracey linked her arm in Tommy's as they walked down the makeshift aisle; Alex and Bailey followed close behind.

The music transitioned and Caroline fought off the butterflies that flapped wildly inside her. Her dad leaned over to kiss her cheek, and whispered, "You ready?" Caroline nodded and gave him one more squeeze before tucking her arm through his. They walked through the old barn doors and out into the warm glow of the setting sun.

Friends and family stood in rows filled with white wooden chairs, heads turned toward the bride and her father. Caroline smiled at a relative who waved shyly, and continued the slow walk down the grassy aisle strewn with petals. Colorful gerbera daisies were tied to the chairs that lined the aisle, mirroring the bright flowers that dotted the meadow in the farmland.

Her eyes followed the colorful petals up to the altar, where *he* stood.

The sight of Jackson in his black tuxedo nearly took her breath away. Even through the long-sleeved shirt and tuxedo jacket, she could still make out the shape of his well-toned arms and broad shoulders.

Caroline's gaze locked onto his and everything else disappeared—she heard no sounds, saw no faces. There was only the blue of his eyes looking soulfully into hers.

She suddenly realized that she had never felt more at peace in her entire life, had never felt more comfortable, or felt more "right" than she did at that very moment.

Caroline knew that her choice to give herself to this man for the rest of her life was the right one. There were no feelings of doubt. There was no indecision. There were no questions.

This was where she was meant to be. And Jackson was the man she was meant to be with. How they got to this point no longer mattered. It wasn't about the past. It was about their future.

Together.

Forever.

They had both always known it.

And today was just the beginning.

Thank You's

I have to start off with the usual suspects- boyfriend and blake. Who have to deal with my mood swings while I'm trying to write. It's tough trying to tune out my surroundings. It's probably even tougher when you're the surroundings I'm trying to tune out. ha

Once again, thank you times infinity (and beyond!!!) to Cat, Becky, Kristina, Michelle P, Loree and Ali. Your opinions, criticism, edits and notes all helped this book grow into the story it is today. Thank you for helping me write good stories!

To my editor- Pam Berehulke. You push me. You challenge me. You tell me when things suck (and boy do they suck- a lot. Lol) But I appreciate everything you do to help me become a better writer and storyteller. I still have a lot to learn, but I'm getting there. Thank you for your infinite patience and wisdom.

I have to thank my spiritual guru, Cindy. Thank you for your inspiration, wisdom and funny little doodles!! You are amazing.

I never realized when I started this journey that I would meet so many AMAZING Indie authors who would eventually become my friend's as well! I actually became a fan of all of these women before I ~~stalked them~~ forced them to love me. I'm forming a gang. And these bitches are in it! Don't mess with my gang. We have horses. Thank you ladies, for not only writing books that I couldn't put down, but for the support, laughter, encouragement, help, guidance, words of wisdom and mostly for being simply amazing human beings. :) I'm so happy to have met you!
Michelle Warren (author of the Seraphina Parrish Trilogy)
Rachel Higginson (author of The Star-Crossed Series)

Colleen Hoover (author of Slammed)
J.A. Templeton (author of The MacKinnon Curse Trilogy)

Thank you to everyone who encourages me, inspires me and tells other people to buy my books. You are invaluable to me as a writer. I can't keep writing if no one buys my books. Well, I can, but um... I couldn't make a living doing it and that would sorta suck- lol. So a special thank you goes out to Liz for always asking "when is the next book coming out???" and being overly excited about everything I write. And to a few book bloggers- for being so amazing and wonderful... Sabrina (paranormal reads), Alishia (treasured tales for young adults) and Kristina (mera's ya book blog) - I can't thank you enough for the support you've given and continue to give me!! And to Rehab, for all of those last minute catches, questions and help. You're the best! :)

2551409R00126

Printed in Great Britain
by Amazon.co.uk, Ltd.,
Marston Gate.